SANDSTORM

A Dystopian Science Fiction Story

Book 1
By
T.W. Piperbrook

T.W. Piperbrook

www.twpiperbrook.com
www.facebook.com/twpiperbrook

Cover Design
Jeff Brown Graphics

Typography
Alex Saskalidis, a.k.a. 187designz

Editing & Proofreading
Cathy Moeschet

Technical Consultant
John Cummings

Formatting
Streetlight Graphics

Preface

Writing ideas come from the strangest places.

Sometimes they creep into our heads while we are on the cusp of sleep. Other times they tug at our subconscious as we go about our normal routines. In this case, the idea for Sandstorm came from a song title, which spawned a full-fledged world, filled with characters and a premise that I couldn't ignore.

As the idea solidified, I envisioned a colony on a harsh desert planet called Ravar, its members cut off from their counterparts on Earth and forced to make do with limited resources. Over time, and with no communication from the supply ships or from Earth, the colonists accepted that perhaps this new planet was their home, and that they weren't leaving.

New caste systems emerged. Stories and rumors developed into truths. And new generations would be taught the most important thing they needed: to survive.

The SANDSTORM series is the story of a young woman on a harsh planet, trying to provide for her family, but it is also the story of a group of outcasts, forced to come together and fight for the only world they know.

Sometimes our greatest expectations are subverted, and we are forced to make do with what life throws at us. SANDSTORM is a very different story than anything I've written, but it reminds me of the situations we face every day.

On a desert planet. With a lurking evil. You'll see what I mean.

I hope you enjoy SANDSTORM Book 1.

Tyler Piperbrook
May 2018

Prologue

S OMETHING HISSED AT AKRON.

He lifted his torch higher, inspecting the gloomy walls of the cave. Shadows grew and fled on the red, sloping stone on either side of him. Somewhere in the darkness above him, wings fluttered. He flicked his eyes upward, watching a bat's shadow flit from one perch to another.

Another, louder hiss bounced off the walls. Something he couldn't see was giving him a warning.

From outside, he heard the howl of the wind and the pelting debris from the sandstorm, from which the cave sheltered him.

His eyes searched the darkness.

Several crevices in the walls spoke of hiding places from which something might spring. But Akron couldn't see what he'd alerted. He clutched the long knife in his hand as a thin scrape echoed around him. Sweat traced trails down Akron's cheeks — sweat he was afraid to wipe. The humid cave felt even hotter.

Another hiss. A slither.

He turned.

A snake slid from the shadows, flicking its tongue as it exposed its venom-filled fangs. The light of Akron's torch reflected off its black, oval eyes and its brown body. Akron froze with fear. He recalled the last time he had encountered a similar reptile. The venomous, six-foot-long creature had slid out at him before he'd had a chance to retaliate, striking the top of his boot. Those twin marks — still visible on the worn leather — should've warned him to stay away from the caves.

And yet here he was.

Slowly, the snake coiled, rubbing its keeled scales together. It inflated its body in a gesture of attack. He had seen several such creatures strike the colonists unaware, sending them into sicknesses that caused fiery pain and death. Those people had spent their last moments gasping for air, whispering for someone in the heavens to save them. Akron didn't wait for a dose of deadly venom. Stepping forward, he hacked downward in a quick swing as the snake leapt.

Blade cleaved flesh.

The reptile's head fell.

A last hiss was cut short as the snake's mouth opened and closed and its tongue flicked. The back end of its body twisted angrily, following a chain of commands from its separated brain.

Akron blew a relieved breath and stared at the dead animal for a long second. The torch cast shadows that could easily be another menacing, deadly creature, come to bite him. It took him several moments to convince himself the danger was over.

Bending down, he speared the animal's head, lifted it up, and carried it to the wall, finding a small crevice where he could stuff it. Thick boots or not, he didn't need to chance stepping on its still-venomous head.

Returning to the snake's body, he realized his luck. The six-foot animal was one of the largest he'd seen recently. Its meat would feed him a day or two — enough that he could spend the rest of his trip exploring. The snake was deadly, but delicious.

Unslinging his pack from his shoulders, he tucked the snake's body into his game bag.

The wind continued howling outside, close enough that

he could hear it, and still feel a faint gust of it as he traveled deeper and away from it.

Akron held his torch high, stepping even more carefully than before. The light revealed the cave's giant, sloping red walls. Some places were smooth, but others were craggy, or recessed deep into places he couldn't see, home to other reptiles and insects, some of which could be just as deadly. Akron knew better than to stick his hand in any of those holes.

He'd learned a lot of things, in his twenty years on his home planet of Ravar.

Ever since he was a teenager — old enough to ignore his parent's warnings and the laws — Akron had traversed the two enormous, cave-filled formations jutting out of the desert on Ravar's surface, creating protective walls on either side of his colony of Red Rock. In the times of his great-grandfather, the colonists had mined the caves, extracting metals and other things of value that could be traded or exported. Old, gaping slashes told the tale of their hard work, all those years ago.

Now, the caves were forbidden.

Generations ago, Akron's people had lost contact with Earth's supply ships. Most speculated Earth was dead. The more cynical of the colonists guessed that the mining mission had been aborted, and a decision had been made to strand the settlement. Whatever the case, The Heads of Colony warned the colonists away from the dark, winding caves. Too many of the early colonists had fallen to their deaths, been trapped, or gotten lost. Even if The Heads of Colony hadn't ordered people away, most were scared by stories of vicious, cave-dwelling animals, or warded off by the humidity and hot temperatures in the caves' many tunnels. The punishment of the loss of a week's crops wasn't enough to outweigh Akron's curiosity.

He'd never been caught, and he didn't plan to be.

Akron preferred the solace of the caves to the loud, abrasive tones of his people, chatting about the wives they'd take, or the game they'd kill. Most in his colony made him uncomfortable. Out of the two thousand people among whom he lived, Akron had few acquaintances, and fewer friends.

Sometimes he slipped to the edges of conversational circles, listening to people talk of the day's heat, or the Green Crops — none of which were green enough — that grew by the southern bank of the colony's river. Occasionally, he'd add something, but too many conversations ended after he spoke, with people either shuffling away or ignoring him. Few sought him out for anything other than a passing question. Akron's lack of confidence might as well have been drawn on his forehead.

His parent's pressures didn't help.

They wanted him to marry. They wanted grandchildren. It wasn't that Akron didn't dream of finding a woman, as well, but his few attempts at conversing with the young females gathering water down by the river were followed by awkward silences. The best he'd received was polite laughter.

And so he'd thrown himself into his exploration.

The caves didn't ignore him when he talked. They didn't smirk when he went past. And they held secrets of which he could only fathom. He'd dreamt about exploring them ever since he'd taken his first steps outside his mud brick house and saw the red, massive formations looming high above him on either side of the colony, like the twisted appendages of some fantastic creatures, planting their massive girth into the sand. He felt as if he was one of the first colonists, before Earth had abandoned them, or died.

One day, he'd make a discovery that would change the way the colonists felt about him. No one would ignore him when he brought back something that changed their lives. It might be worth the risk of breaking the rules.

He would be a hero, hailed by everyone.

He followed the cave until the ceiling recessed, the path grew narrower, and he had to bend down to walk. He could barely hear the wind outside. He had entered the formation through one of the caves at the bottom, away from the cliffs on top, where The Watchers looked out over the colony, scanning for danger, or ensuring colonists like him didn't enter. Most of the other colonists were probably hunkered down, protecting their families from the raging storm. Akron had told his parents he'd been staying with a friend. He had covered his whereabouts.

Akron stuck his torch and knife ahead of him, fitting his limber frame between a few rocks that might have been too wide for a bigger man. His scrawny body—a source of self-consciousness on the outside—was a boon in here.

He kept going as the tunnel wound in a new direction, keeping an eye out for snakes. Occasionally, he heard the flutter of another bat, or the scurry of some cave lizard, moving quicker than the eye could focus. Every so often, he encountered the small bones of a desert rat, or a dust beetle that was several times the size of his head. The tick of those creatures' legs always gave him a fright as they clacked through the tunnels.

Eventually, the rusted red walls curved wider, and his footsteps echoed over crushed stone. On the wall, Akron found a familiar triangular marking he'd made on some earlier trip, faded with time. He'd never seen anyone venture down here to see those markings. Even if they did, they couldn't prove who left them. He shined his torch on the floor, looking for a loose rock with which to retrace the symbol. Most of the stones were too small. Eventually, he located a larger rock that appeared loose in the wall. He pried it free.

A couple more fist-sized stones fell underneath the first rock.

Then a few more.

Akron frowned as a hole appeared in the wall that he'd never noticed. He held up his torch. The exposed hole was dark, about the size of his head, and ran farther than he could see. It looked like the stones had been piled there. Another cave?

Akron pulled away more fist and head-sized rocks from the pile, taking care for critters that might be hiding. Soon, he'd removed all the rocks and piled them up next to the nearby wall, revealing a space big enough to crawl through.

Getting on his hands and knees, Akron scooted through the small passage, balancing his knife and his torch. If he had been claustrophobic, he might've turned around, but Akron kept going. The walls pressed against his shirt until he bent down and was sliding on his stomach. He had almost enough time to question whether what he was doing was a good idea when he came out on the other side of the passage, standing in another cave.

The new cave was twice as big as the one in which he'd been traveling.

A feeling of elation washed over Akron as he realized he'd discovered a new passage.

The cave was humid, littered with rocks, and smelled of rodent scat. How long had it been since anyone traveled it? Akron felt as if he was on the verge of a greater discovery. Excitedly, he looked left and right before choosing a path to the left. He scanned for evidence of other's travels, but saw nothing except the occasional rodent skeleton and some animal tracks.

The tunnel took a steep, downward slope, and the air got warmer. A strange smell hit his nose. He knew that animals often sought shelter in the caves after they'd been wounded. He looked for a corpse, but didn't find one. The tunnel felt immeasurably deep, as if he was headed far underneath the bowels of Ravar, far from his people, far from anything he'd ever known.

He clutched his knife as perspiration dotted his face.

Bugs skittered away on the walls. Rats fled the torchlight. Unease washed over Akron as he studied some of the deep, dark crevices on either side of him, which were deeper than any in the cave in which he'd traveled. Anything could hide in there. Rounding a curve in the tunnel, he found himself in a new, drier passage.

Akron held up his torch.

He had entered an enormous, cavern-sized chamber. The space before him felt wider than a whole row of the mud brick houses in the colony. The dark ceiling was well beyond his torch light. As he took a few more steps, he realized the middle of the floor was level with where he traveled, but on each side of the room, the ground sloped up to ledges he couldn't see.

Akron swallowed and scanned the ground in front of him.

His heart hammered.

Piles of a dusted, waste-like substance were everywhere. Parts of it were black, or brown, but other parts were gray.

But that wasn't the most alarming thing.

Protruding from some of the ashen, waste-like piles were human bones.

Choking on his vomit, Akron turned and ran.

Fear propelled his footsteps as he retreated from the cavern and into the smaller passage that had led him here. His hands shook on his torch and knife. The shadows around him shrank and grew. Hot sweat poured down his face, blurring his vision as something scraped behind him.

He spun.

Something was following him.

Something he couldn't see.

Akron ran faster.

He had only gone a few more steps when one of the shadows came alive and at him. Akron cried out. Too late, he raised his blade. A blinding flash of pain coursed through his skull. His torch flew from his hands.

His last thought was that he'd never tell anyone what he had found.

Akron died before he fell.

Chapter 1: Neena

HOLD STILL... HOLD STILL...

Neena gritted her teeth as she slowly cocked back her spear, watching the Rydeer. The lean, four-legged animal stood sideways at the crest of the dune, the sun shining off its ratty coat. It cocked its antler-less head as it appraised something in the distance. A faint wind blew from behind. Were it not for the breeze, disguising Neena's smell, and the dusted dunes that hid her approach, the animal might be a klick away by now.

It was a lucky find, as long as she killed it.

She clutched the spear tight and slowly moved it backward, gathering her strength for a powerful throw. The beast was close enough that she should be able to land the spear in its shoulder, puncturing its heart or lungs. But if she moved noticeably, she'd spook the creature and miss. Each pang of hunger would remind her that she'd failed not only herself, but also her brothers.

A flash of movement caught her eye.

Neena halted as a smaller creature bounded to the top of the hill, bleating and nuzzling the larger beast. It perked its ears and stamped its spindly legs. A fawn.

Neena gripped her spear, but she didn't throw it.

The fawn wouldn't survive more than a day, if she killed its mother.

Watching the small, rambunctious beast, she couldn't imagine causing its death, or bringing it back after she killed what might be its only relative. Survival was one thing.

Cruelty was another.

Hating her predicament, she relaxed her grip on her spear, but she didn't lower it. As scrawny as the mother was, it would feed her, Raj, and Samel for a long time. It would be hard work dressing it, bagging it, and carrying it back, but she'd do what she could. Neena steadied herself as she decided on a throw to which she couldn't commit.

A gust of wind distracted her.

Neena spun.

A cloud of debris swirled in the distance, picking up speed.

Not just a small wind.

A sandstorm.

Her heart hammered as she watched the spiraling mass of dust and sand that already encompassed most of the horizon. Often, she received an earlier prediction: the slow pickup of the wind, debris swirling close to the ground, or sand rats skittering into hiding. Not today.

Turning, she saw the frightened Rydeer and its fawn bound off. The fawn's frantic bleats echoed down the other side of the dune, and then they were gone.

Dammit.

Neena frantically searched the area, finding nothing but dusty dunes. She was in a section of desert with no nearby caves, or large rocks behind which to hide. Several days ago, she'd left her colony, Red Rock, searching between the crevices of a few larger clusters of rocks, and the red, adobe formations that poked up from the desert. She'd found only a scant few plants to uproot and bring back. Finally, desperation had forced her into an area thick with dunes. She'd traveled for a while without finding anything.

That's when the brown, matted Rydeer crested the hill.

And now it was gone, and she was in danger.

Loosening the shawl around her neck, she wrapped it

tightly around her face, leaving an opening for her eyes, and lowered her goggles.

The building winds lifted the sand from the north. In moments, it would be upon her.

A warning from her dead father came back to her.

Traveling on the leeward side of a dune will get you buried. If you can't find shelter, get to high ground.

She looked up at the dune next to her, noting her precarious position. Plunging her spear into the sand, she started up the incline, using her weapon for balance. The sand grabbed her boots with each step, but the screeching wind drove her onward. When she reached the top of the dune, she hunkered down, spun, and faced the storm. A wall of sand loomed a hundred yards away. Some of the sandstorms on her home planet only lasted a few minutes, but others lasted hours, or days. The severest storms spanned a wide enough area that they might reach her colony, three days away.

She hoped this wasn't one of the latter storms.

Scanning the sky to catch her bearings, she found the two moons, visible over Ravar at this time of day. The only thing worse than getting stuck in a storm was getting lost in one.

And then the storm was upon her.

The wind screamed.

Debris pelted her skin.

Neena pressed her shawl tight against her mouth as the sand pummeled her goggles, rifled her hair, and tore at her clothes. The sand felt like a thousand tiny insects conspiring to bowl her over. Hot sweat plastered her clothes to her body; she struggled to breathe. She'd heard of people suffocating, or peeled alive by the unbidden force of the wind. Some in her colony thought a higher power had created the storms as a display of force, meant to keep her people humble.

At the moment, Neena couldn't disagree.

She felt a surge of anger as she envisioned some of the young men her age in the colony, most of whom would rather drink wastewater than hunt alongside her. They'd purposely waited until she'd left to head out. They were probably safe in some cave, chatting about the game they'd kill and bring back.

Neena was alone, as she usually was.

Worse, she had traveled farther than she intended. All she had were the two flasks of water on her belt and some dried sand rat in the bag on her back.

If her younger brother Raj were older, he would accompany her. But right now, she needed ten-year-old Raj to look after their youngest sibling, Samel, who was six. Their parents were dead, forcing Neena to fulfill a hunter's role.

If something happens to me, at least Raj will keep Samel safe, she thought.

A furious gust of wind ripped away that thought. She slammed her spear into the ground and clutched it tightly, coughing out some sand that found its way past her shawl.

Thunder split the air.

A new, stabbing fear overtook her.

If lightning struck, she would have to change her strategy. More of her father's sage advice came back to her.

Lightning can prove fatal if you are up too high.

Neena shuddered. Watching for streaks of light across the sky, she couldn't bury the fear that she might die before she made it home.

Chapter 2: Raj

RAJ WIPED THE SWEAT FROM his brow as he filled his bucket in the river. Looking left, he stared down the long, winding bank of the river that ran south of Red Rock colony, running from west to east, where men, women, and children huddled, dipping buckets in the water, chatting. A few young kids splashed each other. Others played with sticks. Across the river, five hundred men and women tended the long, expansive rows of green vegetation hearty enough to grow there. A few of the women sang while they worked, their soft, lilting songs carrying over the water as they maintained the crops. More men stood on the edges of the rows, counting the crops they put in their carts.

The wooden bridge that led from one side to the other was filled with people, skirting around each other, or talking. A young couple looked down into the calm water, probably staring at their reflection, as Raj often did when he didn't have chores to do.

Raj changed his focus to the towering, red cliffs that hung high above the eastern side of the colony. A similar formation sat on the colony's western border, providing a two-sided, protective barrier around the large colony, with the river to the south, and the hunting deserts to the north.

Movement drew his attention to one of the formations.

On one of the highest ledges, the silhouette of one man walked toward another, waving his hands in a gesture Raj couldn't make out. Raj frowned as the two men turned in the same direction, pointing.

Raj tightened his grip on his bucket.

Together, the two men walked along a narrow ledge and joined some others, all of whom gestured similarly.

It didn't take a genius to guess what was going on.

The Watchers had seen a storm.

If Raj were privileged enough to be on top of the cliffs, he would've heard what they were saying. But those cliffs, with their multitude of caves and steep ledges, were off limits to most of the colonists — a misplaced step could lead to death, or at best, a broken limb. In the days past, his ancestors used to mine the tunnels, but now The Heads of Colony only let The Watchers up there. Raj squinted through a growing glare as the guarding men walked around a curved mountain ledge and out of sight.

The men were probably gauging the distance and severity of the storm. From up on the ledges, Raj had heard, a person could see almost eighty klicks away. The question was: would The Watchers blow the horn once or twice? A single, urgent note meant the storm was coming quickly. Two rapid notes meant he had time to prepare.

Raj had seen plenty of storms in his ten years. The worst storms leveled the weakest of the mud brick homes, causing damage and death. Others were little more than a nuisance. Judging by the men's reactions, he had a bad feeling about this one.

Raj looked behind him, opening his mouth to call out for his brother.

Samel was gone.

Panic struck Raj as he looked up and down the riverbank. He'd only turned his back for a few moments. Or had it been longer? Pulling his half-full bucket from the water, Raj stood. He scanned behind him, up the long, straight path cut by the boots of the many colonists, which branched off into smaller paths leading between the clusters of mud brick homes.

No Samel.

He glanced west, past a bunch of people he didn't recognize, and then back to the towering red cliffs on the other side of the colony, even though Samel knew better than to venture up onto either of those gigantic formations.

"Samel?" he called.

Raj walked down the riverbank to the east, weaving around several groups of chatting people as he searched for his brother. He'd lost count of the number of times he'd told him to stay near. Where was he?

He passed a group of laughing women, holding buckets or cradling babies. A few glanced casually in his direction before tending their children. Raj kept on, weaving around several more groups of people — a few hunters carrying the usable remains of a Rydeer, a man sharpening a spear, and a woman washing some garments. The screams of happy children reached his ears. No one knew what was coming.

But Raj did.

He walked faster as his nervousness grew.

Raj crashed into something. Water sloshed from his bucket, spilling onto a bearded man's clothes.

"Watch yourself, runt!"

Raj righted the bucket, but not before he'd spilled most of what he had. Startled, he looked from the bucket to the large man into whom he'd crashed. The man gave him an angry look that displayed what he might've done if Raj was older. He barged off.

Raj kept going, finding his way among crowds of people that were too thick to see around. He passed a group of children rolling rocks into a larger pile, laughing as the stones clinked together. A few more played games in the sand. Midday was always crowded by the riverbanks. If Raj hadn't agreed to do chores for Helgid in the morning, he would've come earlier, but in exchange for his help, Helgid had agreed to cook him and Samel lunch. It was a good barter.

Samel had begged to come.

And now he'd run off.

Raj felt a sting of anger. He wouldn't be so quick to bring his little brother next time. He had just skirted around a huddle of older women when he heard commotion farther down the winding banks. Away from some of the older people, a group of children circled around something. Raj frowned as he lugged his heavy bucket toward them, the remaining water sloshing from side to side.

"Go ahead, do it!" a dirt-faced boy cried to someone in the middle of the circle.

"Come on!" cried another.

Raj recognized a few boys his age, or a little older. A bad feeling grew worse as he heard a familiar voice. *Samel's*. Raj dropped the bucket, running toward the fringes of the group in time to watch the boys burst into laughter, covering their mouths and pointing.

"What's going on?" he asked, pushing some of the boys aside.

Samel stood in the center of the circle, an uncertain look on his face as he stared at the ground. A sleek, black scorpion ran near his boots, pincer poised.

"Pick it up, Samel!" one of the older boys cried. "It won't hurt you!"

In mock demonstration, one of the boys darted in, making a swooping motion.

The scorpion spun to face the newcomer, arcing its pincer. The boy leapt backward. Spinning, the scorpion refocused on Samel, who watched it with hesitation and more than a little fear.

"Come on, Samel!" yelled another boy. "Pick it up!"

Feeling the pressure of a half-dozen older boys, Samel bent toward the vicious creature, reaching out his hand.

"Don't do it, Sam!" Raj yelled.

Before anyone could stop him, Raj pulled a sheathed knife from his side, ran into the circle, and pushed his brother away. He bent and stabbed the scorpion to the ground, dead. Ooze dripped from its pierced middle. He pulled the blade free, watching its body sag and its pincer go lifeless.

"Are you okay, Sam?" he asked his little brother, waiting for an answer before he felt relief.

"I'm fine, Raj," Samel answered, as Raj wrapped a protective arm around him.

Raj had seen too many people die when they'd had a reaction. That didn't mean Samel would, but it wasn't a risk anyone should take willingly, and certainly not at the behest of a half-dozen bored boys.

"Let's get out of here," Raj said, staring furiously at the slack-jawed boys in the circle.

Disappointment crossed more than a few faces as they realized the fun was over.

"What the hell?" shouted one of the older boys, a freckled kid with long, brownish hair, a boy named Bailey.

Raj took a step to leave the circle, but Bailey got in the way, glaring menacingly. His eyes flicked to the blade in Raj's hand.

"Are you threatening us with that knife, orphan boy?"

Raj stared at him without answering.

"I asked you a question," Bailey said.

"The sting could've killed him," Raj answered through gritted teeth, as if he needed to explain.

"I pick them up all the time," Bailey said with a coy smirk. "They're harmless."

"Out of my way," Raj said, waving his knife.

Edging in, a kid with a pointed nose said, "Maybe it

would've made a man out of him, instead of a sissy like you."

Bailey laughed.

"Move!" Raj demanded.

"Or what?" Bailey watched him. "You'll send your boyish sister after us?"

"Maybe he'll send his old hag-lady friend." Another kid laughed.

"Are you bringing back water so she can cook lunch?" asked the boy with the pointed nose. "A pair of sissies, raised by a man-girl and an old woman."

"No wonder your father left," sneered Bailey.

Raj's pulse pounded behind his eyes. He took a step toward Bailey, still clutching his knife, pressing close enough that he could smell the sand rat on the boy's breath.

"What are you doing, Raj?" Samel cried.

"Yeah, what are you doing, orphan boy? Are you going to cut me?" Bailey smirked as he stood his ground.

Out of the corner of his eye, Raj saw several of the other kids inching closer, their hands moving toward their blades. Too late, he realized he had made a mistake. He'd never take them all out, knife or not. He held Bailey's glare, clutching his blade and preparing for a fight he wouldn't win.

A long, blaring horn blew.

The kids in the circle looked around, confused. A few of them spun and stepped back. Bailey's stare broke as he looked from Raj to the cliffs, glimpsing The Watchers hurrying down the paths at the top of the red rocks. A man held his curved instrument in the air, blowing a loud, droning note.

"A storm!" one of the dim-witted boys cried.

Near the river, people scrambled and pulled their buckets from the water. A few of the boys scattered, making for the path that cut between the mud brick houses, or separating down different alleys.

Raj looked back at Bailey, who held his ground, his sneer stuck to his face. "This isn't over," he promised, jabbing a threatening finger before breaking off with the rest of his friends.

Raj stood for a moment, shaking.

"Come on, Raj!" Samel cried, grabbing his brother's arm and breaking him from his angry trance. "We have to get home!"

Instinct kicked in, and Raj moved.

Together, they ran, scooping up the bucket Raj had dropped and veering toward the path, joining a cluster of other running colonists.

Chapter 3: Neena

S AND AND DEBRIS PELTED NEENA'S body, stinging her skin beneath the thin fabric of her shirt and pants. She squinted, afraid that the storm would rip away her goggles, exposing her eyes, or that it would tear away her shawl and fill her mouth and ears with sand. Every so often, she let a hand off her spear and pulled her clothing tighter. Heart pounding, she stared through the enormous brown cloud around her, watching the sky for flashes of light that would force her to reconsider her position. As blinding as the storm was, lightning could cut through it.

By the time that she saw lightning, she might be dead.

A rumble of thunder emanated from the sky, piercing the wind around her and sending rippling premonitions through the ground. After what felt like forever, the wind subsided a notch and the sand settled into swirling pockets that hovered over the surface of the uneven, eroded dune on which she perched. A lull. No lightning had struck, but given the intensity of the storm, it might.

Neena needed shelter.

Pulling her spear from the sand, she headed down the dune, navigating through a lingering film of dust and debris as she retraced her path. Of course, her footprints were gone. She no longer saw the twin moons, or even the sun, all of which were hidden by the clouded landscape. The dunes around her were silhouettes, shaved down by the force of the wind. A few of the smaller ones had thinned so much that they were only bumps on the landscape.

She recalled what she knew of the area. She had only been this way a few times, and always out of desperation. This was one of the driest regions of Ravar, filled with only dunes and endless sand. The Heads of Colony forbade it. Areas like this were desolate and prone to death — a hunter was likely to die of thirst before making it out. All the hunters stayed away from it.

At the time, she had thought that might give her an advantage.

Instead, it left her farther from home.

She hadn't seen any other hunters since a day ago, when she had encountered a group on a hilltop, searching through some red, adobe formations. Of course, she had avoided them. None of the hunters respected her. None had ever broken the rules of Red Rock out in the desert, but she knew how quickly hunger could turn to desperation. She wouldn't risk interacting with them.

Neena clamped her mouth shut beneath her shawl, breathing through her nose. Every few steps, she reached up with her free hand, smearing the sand away from her goggles. She scoured what little landscape she could see, hoping she might find a large, sheltering rock, or a formation.

Rounding the corner of a large, sandy dune, she found something else instead.

A body.

Neena's heart raced as she saw a person lying facedown in the sand.

Whoever it was looked dead. She stabbed her spear in and out of the ground as she moved faster, heading for the fallen figure.

Whoever it was, the person couldn't have been there long. They were covered in sand, but they weren't buried.

Neena was positive she would've noticed a body if she had passed it earlier. Unless the wind uncovered it.

She looked around, as if she might spot more of the hunters she'd seen a day ago, but she saw no one.

The whistling breeze warned that the storm wasn't finished. Dipping her head against a pelt of sand, she approached the motionless, fallen body. It looked about a man's size.

"Hello?" she called.

No answer.

"Hello?" she asked again.

She gripped her spear and waited longer for a response. No movement, no sound. A realization hit her.

The man wore darker clothing than her, with more pockets and folds. In fact, she'd never seen garments as strange.

It couldn't be a hunter from Red Rock.

Who was it?

Neena's breath caught in her throat. When she was younger, she'd heard whispers that several, strange people had made a long, hot trip through several deserts, reaching her people and visiting The Heads of Colony. That supposed visit had been almost a decade ago. The Heads of Colony had kept the contents of those conversations mostly private, except to tell the colonists they were in no danger. She remembered the cloud of fear that hung over the colony after that visit. Eventually, weeks turned into months, and the story of the visitors became legend, just like the stories of the supply ships from Earth that used to grace the skies.

Outside of that, she'd never heard of anyone visiting Red Rock. And she'd certainly seen no one.

Was this one of those same, strange people?

Whoever he was, he needed help.

Neena took several careful, tentative steps toward him

as she kept an eye on her surroundings. Where there was one stranger, there might be more. She saw no one else.

Bending down, she poked the man with a finger.

He didn't move.

Was he unconscious, or dead?

Slowly, carefully, she tucked her hands under the man's side and tried rolling him. She waited for a grunt or a moan—something that would indicate she'd aggravated a wound. Or entered a trap. Looking around, she saw no one. Finally, she got the man on his back.

The man remained silent and still, with his eyes closed. His dark hair was plastered to his head by a dried gash of blood on his forehead; strange markings were imprinted on his temples. The markings appeared as if they'd been burned in.

What were they?

Deep in the distance, a wall of debris moved in their direction. She needed to check the man's breathing and see if he was alive. If he wasn't, she needed to move before—

The man moaned.

Neena jumped back and fell on her butt, avoiding his reaching hands.

"Stay back!" she warned, getting her spear in front of her.

The man's moan turned into an indecipherable mumble. He sat up, coughing, and opened his eyes. His sand-crusted face was filled with fear. When he saw Neena, he leaned back and thrust his hands in front of him. It looked like he was afraid—afraid of *her*. Neena kept her spear pointed.

"Who are you?" she demanded.

The man didn't answer.

"Can you understand me?"

The man coughed through a response. His eyes were blue and wide. Feeling the weight of Neena's unanswered question, he pointed at his throat.

Slowly, Neena pulled one of her flasks from her belt and scooted toward him, clutching her spear tightly. She kept her body at a distance, where he couldn't easily attack, and held out the flask. Cautiously, the man reached out and took hold of it, pulling it toward him. He uncapped it and sipped with the vigor of a person who hadn't drunk in a while. After several large gulps, he handed it back, carefully.

"Thanks," he croaked, retracting his hands.

"What's your name?" she asked.

"Kai." His voice was hoarse, barely audible.

"Where are you from?"

"New Canaan," he managed.

"New Canaan?" Neena furrowed her brow. "I haven't heard of it."

Kai stared at her, as if he was figuring out where she'd come from. Or maybe he didn't know where he was. "Who are you?" he croaked.

"My name is Neena. I'm from..." she stopped herself before revealing anything. The wind whipped her attention back to the returning cloud of dust and debris. "We have no more time for questions, Kai. Can you walk?"

"I-I think so," he answered.

"We have to find shelter, or we'll get caught in the storm again."

Kai dragged a hand over his sandy face.

"Don't rub your eyes," she warned. "We'll flush them out when we get somewhere safe." Instinctively, she looked down at her flasks, thinking about her water supply.

"Okay."

Unslinging her bag, she took out her spare pair of goggles, getting close enough to hand them to him. She didn't trust him fully, but right now, something more pressing was coming. "Take them. They'll protect your face."

Kai nodded appreciatively, reaching out to accept them. "Thank you."

He slipped the goggles over his head. Shakily, he found his footing. Thunder rumbled in the distance, making him jump. He took a faltering step. He seemed delirious and dehydrated. Whoever he was, he didn't seem like he was in a condition to hurt her, that was for certain.

Lowering her guard, she said, "Here, let me help you," and offered an arm.

"Thanks," he said.

"I haven't seen lightning yet," Neena called over the increasing gale. "But that doesn't mean it isn't coming."

Together, they started moving. Another, massive rumble reverberated off the ground, closer this time.

Responding to his terrified expression, she explained, "Thunder!"

Kai said something she couldn't hear, his eyes growing wide. Tilting her head, she asked him to repeat it. Her heart pounded as she made out the words.

"It's not thunder! It's coming for us! Run!"

Chapter 4: Raj

Raj and Samel fled north on the worn path, running past several people who scrambled for their children, or called urgent warnings to relatives. Throngs of people hastily carried their buckets up the pathway, spilling water. Men and women grabbed laundry from the lines. A few people stopped to assist the elderly, leading them inside their mud brick homes as the long, urgent note of the horn blew again. The wind had already picked up, whistling around the cracks and crevices of the square buildings, keening in a way that reminded Raj of the death and destruction that similar storms had caused.

The last sandstorm had claimed five lives. By the looks of it, this one might take more.

The path ahead was quickly filling with people. Raj and Samel's home was in the middle of the colony — halfway between the river and the rows of houses facing the northern desert. Helgid lived a few rows farther north.

"Come on!" he told Samel, weaving off the path and cutting between several houses, dodging swarms of colonists who had the same idea to take a shortcut. Raj bumped shoulders with several frantic people. Unlike the man who scolded him earlier, all of them were too preoccupied to notice.

A few excited cries called Raj's attention west, where a wall of debris lifted high above the houses, engulfing the northern limits of the colony and obscuring the first of the homes. The sandstorm looked like a gigantic, dirty blanket, looming over the colony and folding it in a suffocating embrace. A swell of panic coursed through Raj as the rising wind kicked up around him, stinging his face. Reaching into his pocket, he pulled out his goggles.

"Get yours on, Sam!" he called.

Skirting through another alley, Raj changed course.

"Where are we going, Raj?" asked Samel, struggling to keep up.

"We don't have time to get to Helgid's! We have to get home!"

Racing through a few more alleys, they reached their house — a ramshackle building in a row of others — and hurried inside. Operating on muscle memory, Raj collected their cookware, tied it up in a blanket, and placed it near the sturdiest wall. He repeated the precaution with their piles of clothing, before placing their bedrolls in the middle of the room.

With their goggles pressed firmly over their faces, Raj and Samel huddled on their bedding. Raj no longer heard the cries of the colonists herding their children, or the elderly scuttling to safety. It was as if everyone else in the colony had been swept away. Or maybe the opposite was true, and he and Samel were in some strange place, whisked far from the colony.

The wind shrieked like a dying, terrified woman. A particularly loud gust rattled the door in its frame, making Samel shiver.

The house's entrance was built in an easterly direction to block the prevailing winds, and all of the houses had the advantage of the red rock formations on either side of the colony. Still, the sandstorm felt like a raging monster, finding its way through crevices Raj didn't know existed.

Holding his brother, he recalled a vicious storm that had torn through the colony years ago, knocking over several houses and burying a child Samel's age. Raj remembered the wails of that child's mother as they pulled her son's lifeless, sand-covered body from the wreckage. It almost didn't seem right that they had buried him again. The story of that death had weighed on the colonists' shoulders for weeks.

Raj couldn't help but relive that memory now, as he clung to his brother and said a silent prayer to the heavens for protection, even though no one ever answered. When he was younger, his mother had held him in her safe, protective arms, the way he was doing for Samel now. The last time he had seen Mom alive was when she ducked into the house to give birth to Samel.

He recalled the frantic, panicked faces of the healers, and his father's grief-stricken expression when Dad finally came out of the house. At the time, Raj was only four — too young to understand how permanently that day would change things.

It was times like these he missed Mom.

And of course, he missed Dad, too.

All they had left was Neena.

Thinking of his sister, out in the desert and on her own, Raj had another fear. Was she stuck in the storm? Was she waiting it out, like they were?

Wherever she was, he hoped she was safe.

Chapter 5: Neena

NEENA CLUTCHED KAI'S ARM AS they ran. Kai seemed to have found a burst of terrified strength, keeping up with her. Neena had no idea what he feared, but the panic in his eyes made her believe that something worse than a sandstorm was coming. She could no longer see the valley ahead of them, or the dunes toward which they headed.

What was chasing them?

Another rumble reached her ears.

It felt like it was coming from below.

She recalled a nightmare Samel had had a few months ago. He'd woken up, shivering, and Neena had consoled him. He'd told her about a dream he'd had. He'd been out in the desert, with no one around, when the ground opened up, revealing a hole with no bottom. Samel had tried running away, but wherever he went, another hole opened, then another, as if the planet was trying to consume him.

Maybe this was Samel's nightmare come to life.

Neena shuddered as the wind kicked up, blurring their surroundings beyond thirty feet. Something shrieked in front of them. She let go of Kai, put two hands on her spear, and raised it. Animal hooves pounded the sand. A bleat filled the air. Something brown and furred ran in their direction.

A Rydeer.

She had a brief moment to wonder whether it was

the same one she'd seen earlier, before it shot past them, braying and nearly knocking Neena over. Neena cried out in surprise and spun, watching the Rydeer continue in the opposite direction, its hooves beating the sand.

Something exploded from the ground, pitching the Rydeer skyward.

It shrieked in panic and pain.

Through the dust and flying silt, Neena saw something that made her question whether she was living in a nightmare, after all.

An enormous creature—bigger than the mouth of the largest caves she'd seen, long and round enough to fill several tunnels—took the Rydeer up with it. The Rydeer gave a frightful shriek as the creature opened its giant maw, revealing a mouthful of sharp, gigantic teeth, and caught it mid-air, biting down. Hot blood rained down on Neena's face, soaking her goggles and her shawl. Through the blur of sand, wind, and blood, she saw the beast swallow the Rydeer. The enormous creature's shadow loomed over Neena and Kai as it rose higher. Matted, long protrusions unfolded from its scaled body. The protrusions grew rigid and stabbed the air like hundreds of spears.

"Watch out!" Kai screamed over the wind.

Hands pushed Neena to the ground.

She landed on her stomach as a deafening crash pierced the ground behind her, spraying up sand and silt. Her spear skittered away. Looking back toward the boom, she saw an enormous, caving hole in the ground, with sand sliding back into the crevice. The planet felt as if it was pulling in everything around it.

"Come on!" Kai screamed, grabbing her arm and tugging her upright, away from the sliding soil.

"My spear!" she yelled, reaching in the direction of the hole. But it was already gone, or buried.

"Forget it! Come on!"

The ground shook behind them. They moved faster than before, with Kai leading. If Neena hadn't felt the pounding of her heart, or smelled the wet blood on her goggles and shawl, she might've convinced herself she was living a nightmare.

Neena had seen sand rats, Rydeers, and dust beetles the size of her torso, but never anything that could swallow a human in a bite. The Rydeer's dying shriek rang in her head. What was happening?

"Keep moving!" Kai screamed.

She cried out as the ground shook underneath her feet. Her boots lifted and the sand rose. It felt like as if the planet were exploding. Kai tugged her away from a splitting seam coming in their direction. They veered this way and that, tripping every so often, but managing to keep upright.

Kai fell.

His hand ripped from her grasp. Neena cried out as she stopped, reaching for him.

"Come on!"

The seam tore closer—a gaping crevice coming toward them. Finding his arm, she tugged him upright, pulling him back into a frantic run before the sand caved behind them. They changed direction, barely managing to keep ahead of it.

And then they were heading up an incline.

Neena couldn't see the top of the dune, but she kept going, ignoring the pain in her legs, and her heart's frantic thunder. Reaching the highest point, they halted and looked backward.

At any moment, Neena was certain the creature would burst from the ground and engulf them, but all she saw was a swirling wall of debris. The wind shrieked and howled, but the rumbling had ceased.

Leaning over, yelling into Kai's ear over the wind, she asked, "What was that thing?"

"We call it the Abomination."

Neena had no time to question the strange word. "Where did it go?"

"It's having trouble finding us in the storm, but it will keep looking!" he answered. Pulling her head close so she could hear, he said, "We need to keep moving!"

Neena nodded.

She caught a glimpse of Kai's face through the storm. His eyes were terrified slits beneath the goggles. The gash in his forehead had started bleeding again. She wondered what other awful things he had witnessed. She had a feeling she'd find out, before the day was done.

Chapter 6: Gideon

"**B**RACE THE DOOR!" GIDEON CALLED, motioning to two Watchers, who were already hurrying for the long, wooden post next to the open doorway of the Comm Building. They lifted the heavy piece of wood while several other men slammed the door, dulling the wind's scream. The Watchers wedged the board into several wooden grooves, stepping back and wiping the sand from their faces.

A heavy gust of wind drew Gideon's attention to the roof, where something struck the edge of the dome and scraped over the top. A pang of fear he wasn't used to coursed through him.

Looking at the sloping roof's surface, it was easy to spot the years of repair. Some parts of the roof were comprised of the same slate gray stone that made up the rest of the building, but too many sections showed different colors, where they had patched the roof with the same mud brick as the rest of the hovels outside. The enormous, round building was the construct of the first generation — brave men who had forged a path on a new planet. He and his men had kept it stable, but the storm was severe enough that even Gideon worried it might collapse.

The other Heads of Colony — Wyatt, Brody, Saurab, and Horatio — hovered instinctively near the round table in the room's center, watching him. Nearby, The Watchers silently judged the building's stability, with tan, weather-beaten faces. Most had made it down from the cliffs before the storm started. A few had been forced to duck for cover. They were brave men, but the storm had them rattled.

All of Gideon's men knew the protocol for a storm such as this. The best place to be was in the main room, where they could survive underneath the enormous, round table if the roof collapsed. Everyone knew to stay away from the walls, or the private quarters accessed by the doors along the round edges of the main room. Those smaller rooms might easily become their graves.

He appraised the table, around which most of his Heads of Colony instinctively gathered. Around it were two dozen chairs. In its middle was a huge, metal centerpiece—a remnant from the days of the earliest colonists. Gideon traced the contours of the round, strange relic. The piece of metal was covered in small flaps and useless buttons he would never understand. Whenever he looked at it, he envisioned the enormous, rusted satellite dish of which it had been a part.

His father had told him about it. At one time, the dish had been a means of communication between Ravar and Earth, sending signals through some pieces of metal in the sky to the ships, reporting back on the colonists' mission. Over generations, the satellite dish had lost its use, like most of the other things that used to be in the room, scavenged by his ancestors and turned into things of necessity. Long ago, the metal's last scraps had sunk into the sand beneath the other side of the cliffs on the western formation. That area was forbidden, like too many other areas of danger.

Lost in a moment of reflection, Gideon ran his hands over his gray hair. Whenever he looked at the remainder of that relic, he recalled watching his father and his men hovering around the table during sandstorms like these, the way he and his men did now. His father had always kept him close, allowing him to attend every meeting, priming

Gideon for the role that would encompass the rest of his life. Gideon had taken his position seriously, and would continue to do so until his death, just like his father, and his grandfather.

He'd never forget his father's last words as he lay on the bed in his room, dying of old age.

"Preservation at all costs."

A rattling noise distracted him.

Gideon's head jerked to a section of wall by the entrance, where one of the dozen hanging fossils shook. His head Watcher, Thorne, hurried over, adjusting the long, curved, yellowed skull. Thorne's severe expression didn't waver as he rotated the fossil with muscular, tanned arms.

The ancient skull was several times the size of Gideon's head.

He knew those bones almost as well as he knew his own body.

"Should we take it down?" Thorne asked.

Gideon studied the shaking object, and the others next to which it hung. All of the skulls had been there far longer than he had been alive, secured into the walls by pieces of metal that were probably older than the building, and would probably outlast both he and his men.

Each one was different, but no less entrancing. More times than Gideon could count in his childhood, he had stared at those skulls with equal fright and imagination, trying to put flesh over their bones. He had envisioned the animals that had walked around with them, with the heavens only knew how many legs. Each of the skulls contained a multitude of gaping sockets, housing features of which only his ancestors knew.

His eyes riveted on one in particular — an oversized skull with three orifices that might be eyes. A few of the animals appeared similar to the Rydeer that roamed the desert, or even the speckled wolves, but more than a few were decidedly hideous. The shaking skull's jawbone wiggled up and down with some wind that must be getting in through a crevice. Thankfully, that species was dead, or hadn't been spotted in so long that it might as well be, like most of the others.

The harsh environment—and the earliest hunters—had killed them off.

"Sir?" Thorne called over to him, awaiting his command.

Gideon swallowed, feeling a tinge of childhood fright he hated. With the sandstorm raging, it was easy to imagine himself and his men all buried, and some strange, future race digging them up.

"Leave the skulls. They'll be fine," Gideon ordered. "Get back to the table. We should be ready, in case the winds get worse."

Chapter 7: Darius

A CLATTER ECHOED ACROSS THE ROOM.

Darius cursed as he put too much weight on his bad leg, hobbling with his cane over to the workbench. He found a fallen chisel on the ground underneath, rolling back and forth on the floor. He must've missed it. Straining to reach it, he caught hold of it and secured it in one of his bins underneath the thick bench.

He looked around to see if he'd left any other loose objects around.

In various spots across the workbench and on a few other tables that sat alongside the walls of his dirty hovel, piles of heavier tools sat in their usual positions, overlapping or stacked on top of one another. Most were heavy enough that they shouldn't fall. He'd stowed most of the scrap metal away safely. Those metal scraps — artifacts from the days when the supply ships went to and from Ravar — had been pulled from the desert in various scavenging runs throughout the years. Others, he had secretly found in the caves when he was a younger man, before the accident had taken the use of his leg.

The metal served him well while fixing his neighbors' weapons, tools, or cookware, earning him meals to supplement his rations.

Everything seemed stable.

The only thing left on the wall was the long, metal spear that hadn't seen use in more years than he remembered.

A sad, nostalgic feeling coursed through Darius as he remembered the days when he could hunt.

He'd leave it.

If the house caved, he would have greater problems than his old spear.

Huddling down so that he was level with the workbench, Darius found an empty spot and eased into a sitting position. Clutching his cane, his thoughts traveled where they always did, in the midst of such a storm. A tear fell down Darius's wrinkled, sun-spotted cheek as he envisioned Akron's body, long rotted and decayed in some hidden cave.

On most days, his guilt weighed in his stomach, threatening to pull him under. But during sandstorms like these, it was even worse, because Akron had disappeared during one.

Darius hadn't given up hope.

It was his fault Akron had died, and he would make up for it.

One day he'd find the boy's remains and bury them.

Chapter 8: Neena

NEENA AND KAI KEPT A quick pace, stumbling every so often in the heavy wind and sand, pushing through the soreness and the powerful gusts that fought their every step. Neena's body was scraped from her fall. Her legs felt as if they might collapse.

She wished she had her spear.

Even the long, pointed weapon would be useless against a creature as large as the one they'd seen. She pulled her knife from the sheath at her side, realizing how useless it was. It might as well be a grain of sand to the beast. And Kai had nothing but the clothes on his back.

It felt as if they were insects, waiting for a giant boot to squash them.

Neena reached up, smearing some of the dried sand and blood away from her goggles. A coppery odor filled her nose, but she had no time to clean herself or her gear off properly.

They kept running, skirting between desert dunes for longer than she could keep track of, heading in a direction only the heavens knew. Every so often, Neena heard a rumble in the distance, but never as close or as loud. More than once, she looked down at her feet, as if the ground might disappear beneath her, or a gigantic set of sharp, bloodied teeth might emerge and engulf her.

Eventually, after they had run for a long while, the rumbling ceased again, and a large, reddish-brown silhouette appeared through the wind and dust. Four connected, maroon rocks reached into the sky. The segments of stone varied in length, like the enormous, thick palm of a hand and several fingers. Neena recognized the formation.

Her hope renewed.

She passed by the reddish rocks on every hunting trip. Although most of the formation was solid, she knew of a downward outcrop of rock that hid a small cave just big enough to crawl into. She had a memory of going inside the small den with her father on one of her earliest hunting trips.

"This way!" she urged, tugging Kai.

Getting close, Neena weaved around some unattached rocks that surrounded the formation's base. She traveled in a circle until she found the opening. Beckoning, she showed Kai. Together, they huddled down and scooted through the formation's narrow entrance. The cave was small and smelled of animal droppings, but it was a few degrees cooler than the heat of the desert.

And it was out of the storm, and away from the creature.

Neena scurried over loose gravel and rough stone. The ceiling was just high enough that they could walk with their backs bent. Several, smaller holes on the walls spoke of hiding places for desert animals, but Neena saw nothing else in the dim lighting. They stopped and turned. With the walls around them, the keen of the wind fell slightly quieter, but it was still abrasive, battering against the outside of the solid formation.

Sand blasted by the opening. Sticks and pebbles carpeted the cave's first few feet. Neena clutched her knife, her panicked breaths burning her throat.

"Is it gone?" she asked Kai, listening for more rumbles over the wind.

Kai knelt. Cocking his head, he said, "I haven't heard it in a while, but it could be deeper underground. The rumbling is only audible when it gets to the sand's top layers."

"How did it find us?" Neena kept her voice low as she stared through the entrance.

Kai pointed at his boots. "Vibrations," he said. "It followed us."

Neena thought of how the sand rats hid from the storm. They sensed something, even before it was coming. Perhaps this was something similar, though she had trouble fathoming it.

"Can it hear us talk?" she whispered.

"We should be safe if we keep our voices to a whisper, but we shouldn't risk more than that," he said.

Neena nodded. Kai didn't need to tell her twice. Dozens of questions swam into her head. "Where did this thing come from?"

"It lives in the deserts near my colony," Kai said.

"New Canaan?" Neena remembered, still having trouble processing the existence of another colony, let alone the beast. "How far away is that?"

"I don't know anymore," Kai said. "Several days, probably even longer. I lost direction in the sandstorm. The Abomination has followed me, never close, but never far. I haven't been able to lose it."

"All this way, and it is still tracking you?" Neena asked.

"It has taken in a keen interest in me. I wish I could lose the thing." Kai shook his head.

"I've never seen anything like it. And my people haven't, either. At least, I don't think they have." Neena's confusion was written on her face. "I don't understand how something like that could be here."

"Your people are fortunate. Or perhaps they live far enough away that they never had to worry." Kai's expression went grave. Looking out the cave's opening, where the wind whipped past, Kai said, "We should be safer in here, because the rock that makes up this cave is more solid than the sand.

I can't promise our safety, but we are better off here than in the desert."

The pungent odor on her goggles filled Neena's nose. Reaching up, she carefully lifted them off and inspected them. A thick, clear goop was mixed with the Rydeer's blood. Neena had skinned and dressed plenty of animals, but she'd never smelled something so foul.

"What is this?" she whispered, smearing it off on the floor.

Kai looked over, catching sight of the vile substance. "The creature's bile," he whispered gravely. "It helps it swallow its meals."

A panicked fear struck Neena as she reached up, finding some of the substance on her face.

Noticing her expression, Kai said, "You don't have to worry. It's disgusting, but it won't cause you pain."

Kai silently removed his goggles, dusting the sand off. Without the protective mask, or the whipping debris, she got a better look at him. His eyes were blue and intense; his nose was sharp. The strange, curved markings started at his hairline, extending down toward his temples. He was about five years older than her. If she were one of the girls down by the river, she might have called him handsome, if she had time for such thoughts.

Was he one of the strange visitors her people had seen, in that visit years ago?

Too many questions.

The strange word Kai had told her rang in her head. *The Abomination.*

The name was almost as terrifying as the beast she'd seen.

"Earlier, you said that the storm confused the creature," Neena remembered.

Kai nodded.

"But it found the Rydeer," she recalled.

"The Rydeer panicked," Kai said, brushing some of the sand from his face. "It made too much noise. Its bleating and its frantic hooves brought on its death. Or maybe the Abomination got lucky."

Kai tried using his shirt to clean some of the debris near his eyes. He cursed and blinked.

"Take my water," she said, handing over one of her flasks. "But use it sparingly."

"Thanks," he whispered. He tilted his head back, washing some of the sand from his eyes, but careful not to spill too much. "If you hadn't found me, I probably wouldn't be alive."

"Do you have any supplies?" she asked, looking him up and down as if she might've missed something.

"I lost them days ago," Kai said, shaking his head. "I haven't had time to do much more than run. I barely managed to eat and drink. I dug water from tree roots. I ate whatever plants I could find, while I avoided that thing." A gruesome expression took over his face. "A few times, I scared some birds away from a carcass and ate the leftovers. Sometimes the food made me sick, but I did what I had to."

Neena grimaced, but they both knew eating was better than dying.

"Before you found me, I had a sharp stick." Kai patted his pants in confusion, as if the weapon might appear. "I must've lost it when I fell."

Neena nodded. It was probably buried in the desert, where she'd found him. Of course, there was no going back for it now.

Holding up the flask, he asked, "Do you mind if I drink some?"

"Go ahead."

"We should stay hydrated," Kai told her. "We might need to run."

Neena removed her other flask, and they both drank

while the wind shrieked outside. The storm seemed to have intensified. Clouds of dust and sand drifted into the cave, like some translucent monster, swirling around the cave with wispy arms. They put their goggles back on. More questions rattled around Neena's mind.

Before she could voice them, a flash of light illuminated the cave.

The walls around them brightened, revealing a multitude cracks and crevices. Neena looked on either side of them, as if she might find another threat, skulking nearby. Or maybe the lightning attracted the Abomination. She didn't know enough about the monster to be certain of anything.

She recalled her time on the dune, hunkering down and watching for lightning. If only she knew how prescient that thought would be.

But lightning seemed like the lesser worry.

Another grumble sounded from further away.

"Was that it?" she hissed over at Kai, wondering whether she heard something worse than a side effect of the storm.

Kai looked frightened. "I'm not sure, but we should stop talking, in case."

He handed back her flask. Together, they grew silent and listened, and Neena held on to her many questions.

Chapter 9: Gideon

IDEON LOOKED AROUND THE COMM Building at the men gathered around the table. A few of the men turned their heads in unison as the wind shook against the brace holding the door. Others looked at the skulls, a few more of which rattled. If the storm worsened, he would order the strictest precaution and have them hunker down.

Each of the men knew the value of their lives. He and his Heads of Colony were the sand and mud that glued the hovels outside together, turning a crowd of people into a society.

And they had no small duty.

In the aftermath of the storm, they would have tallies to take, crops to count, and buildings to mend. Depending on their fortune—or misfortune—they might have people to bury.

In a way, the storm was only the first of the tests.

To his right, Wyatt, one of his Heads of Colony, stared over at him with a severe expression. He scratched at his long, crooked nose, as he did when he was steeped in worry. Next to him, Brody slid one hand over the other. Both men were skilled in estimations and numbers. Their aptitude would assist Gideon in assessing the damage to the crops. Saurab and Horatio, his other two Heads, studied the strength of the ceiling. After the storm, they would gauge any widespread damage, recruiting volunteers to assist in the repairs.

Watchers filled the rest of the room.

The sweat and stink of a few dozen, anxious men turned a hot space into a sweltering one, but everyone stayed silent. No one complained. They had survived plenty of storms before.

Thorne, Gideon's Head Watcher, looked toward the northern side of the room.

Jutting out from the other side of that door was the prison annex, which extended past the round building. In the days of the first generation, that secured extension had housed extra rations, but now it served a more judicial purpose. When things ran smoothly, most of those dusty, dank cells remained empty. But storms like this taxed even an honest man's heart. If the rations ran thin, some of the colonists might resort to stealing, or breaking the rules.

If things went poorly, Thorne and his Watchers would fill those rooms, under Gideon's jurisdiction.

They would survive, because they had no choice, in this inherited wasteland.

Chapter 10: Darius

T HE TORCH ON DARIUS'S WALL died, leaving him alone and in the dark. He didn't bother relighting it. He knew it would do no good. The flame wouldn't repel the storm, nor would it erase his nightmares, which always seemed to come during storms like these.

For a long time, he stared at the dark walls and listened to the wind battering the outside of his hovel. Eventually, his eyes grew weary, and he closed them.

The next thing he realized, he was in a hazy desert. Darius stiffened and looked around. The ground was made of fine white sand — pure and unblemished, more magnificent than anything he'd seen. Looking down at his boots, it seemed as if he were floating rather than walking. He saw no footprints that showed how he'd gotten here.

Of course, he couldn't see farther than twenty feet through the haze.

Darius's heart rammed against his ribcage as he felt something staring at him from a place he couldn't see. The longer he waited, the more certain he was that an ominous entity lurked nearby. His only thought was to get away from it.

Darius took a step, then another, cutting through the encircling dust. Somewhere in the distance, he heard the howl of the wind, but the haze was surprisingly still, as if he was in some walled-off place, far from the storm, far from everywhere he'd known.

The entity stalked him.

His cane felt immeasurably heavy, pinning him to the ground rather than supporting him. The landscape provided no clues as to where he was. All around him was the nearly impenetrable haze, and the white sand. He might as well be running in a circle.

A gust of gentle wind caressed the back of his neck. Darius shuddered as the hairs above his collar prickled and the cold wormed its way through his skin, bringing a chill to his bones.

Not wind.

An icy breath.

Darius spun, intent on confronting the strange entity, but he saw only dust. It felt as if the landscape was swallowing him, turning him into part of it. He couldn't let that happen.

He needed to escape.

With each step, he felt the entity chasing, grazing the back of his clothing, ready to invade his mouth and nose, ripping away his breath with icy tendrils.

"Leave me alone!" he screamed, thrusting out his cane.

He slashed his free hand through the haze, as if he might be able to break through it.

A glowing white door appeared in front of him.

Darius blinked, as if he might be hallucinating. Or maybe he was being tricked. But the door was there, about ten feet away: bright, impenetrable, and projecting warmth. Slowly, he gained enough courage to walk toward it.

Maybe he'd found a way out.

He forced himself to believe that, as he approached it. He raised his cane, watching the stick pass through the door and disappear. His heart thundered. The door had no physical appearance, other than light. He pulled his cane back, unblemished.

The light rippled.

Darius lowered his cane and took a step back.

A person's face poked through the center of the

door, at eye-level. The person's visage was fuzzy at first, imperceptible. They turned their face, stopping when they found Darius. A pair of white, colorless eyes sat in the middle of featureless skin. Darius tensed. But the person coming through didn't seem threatening.

The person solidified.

They took a step.

Darius's breath caught in his throat.

Akron.

The boy became flesh-colored, skin became skin, and his mouth curved into the same, wide smile that Darius remembered. And then Akron was out of the light and in the desert, standing in front of him.

Darius smiled back at his friend, relief overtaking him. Akron wasn't dead, after all.

He'd found Akron!

He opened his arms as Akron stepped forward to meet him. Darius was inches away from an embrace when the light in the door rippled again, and a bony hand shot out, tugging Akron backward. Akron cried out in terror, horror lighting his face as a dozen more reaching hands came from the light, pawing and groping, pulling him back. He thrust an elbow behind him, trying to break from their clutches.

Darius screamed his friend's name.

He lunged and latched on to the boy's shirt, but the hands on the other side pulled harder, ripping him away. Darius stumbled back. With a soundless thud, he fell onto the white sand.

Akron's face distorted as he fell back through the door. His nose bent and twisted; his eyes bulged and melted. The last thing Darius saw was one of his fingers, reaching out for Darius. With a final, terrified scream, Akron vanished.

The door solidified into a wall of blackness.

Darius woke up with a yell, as the sandstorm continued raging around him.

Chapter 11: Neena

L IGHTNING FLASHED, CUTTING THROUGH THE darkness that enveloped the cave. Each thunderous rumble might be the beast, or it might be the storm. Kai was little more than a shadow sitting next to Neena, visible in those intermittent moments when the cave brightened. They kept mostly still, shifting only when they needed to avoid cramps. Neena kept a cautious eye between Kai and the desert.

With too much time to think and fear, she replayed the events from earlier. She'd never forget the enormous, jagged teeth of the creature, tearing the Rydeer in half, or the gaping hole in the sand, left in its wake. She thought of what Kai had told her. She couldn't imagine surviving a beast as large or as deadly for so long – and especially without water, or a weapon.

Those thoughts led to another that she'd temporarily put aside. She'd lost her main weapon.

My spear.

That last thought hit her so hard and so fast that a pang of grief accompanied her fear. The spear had been her father's. He had left it for her before he departed for the desert for the final time. Now, the weapon was probably buried so far underground that neither person nor beast would come across it again.

She might not miss it for long, before she died.

Looking out at the whipping wind, Neena couldn't

assure herself that she'd survive another day. She no longer had any sense of day or night. With no sun or moons to gauge the time, she could only guess by the temperature.

The heat was fading, which meant night was coming.

The desert nights were as cold as the days were sweltering. Most nights, she slept close to her fires when she was lucky enough to find enough wood to burn, staving off the bitter cold. The few blankets Neena carried in her bag were barely enough to keep her warm.

They remained in place for a long while, listening and watching, until Neena changed positions again. She sat back, clutching her knees and keeping a tight grasp on her knife.

A forgotten feeling struck her.

Hunger.

With all the running and hiding, she'd ignored it. Neena hadn't eaten since morning. She recalled hunkering under the shade of a rock outcropping, consuming a few pieces of sand rat while escaping the bright rays of the sun. She couldn't imagine eating anything now, with the dread of the monster outside, but Kai's warning came back to her: they might need their strength.

Slowly, she removed the pack from her back, feeling around inside. Kai looked over anxiously, thinking she'd heard something. In a flash of light, she signaled she was okay. Feeling around in the dark, her hands came across a few thin blankets and shawls and some empty game bags. Eventually, she found the small pouch containing the last of the meat she'd saved. Digging out some sand rat, she handed it over to Kai. He was surprised, until he realized what she gave him. He took it gratefully, stuffing it into his mouth and chewing wordlessly.

Neena ate some, saving a little.

Together, they consumed the meat in silence, watching the flashes of light through the storm. Another, strange feeling came over Neena.

For too many years, Neena had hunted alone, sharpening her spear in similar caves, collecting her water and her game. It felt good to have someone with whom to share her worries. But she had to remind herself that Kai was a stranger, about whom she knew less than the monster.

Finally, when the chill of the setting sun prickled her arms with goose bumps, Kai leaned over, breaking their silence.

"It is almost night, judging by the cold," Kai whispered, solidifying her guess.

Neena nodded. "That's what I thought, too."

"Abomination or not, I don't think we would have much luck traveling in the storm. The winds will blow out a torch."

"And we will lose direction," Neena finished. Even if she wanted to leave, she couldn't imagine stepping out into the darkness and the wind. Looking in Kai's direction, she asked, "Do you think it will hunt us at night?"

"I don't think it cares about days or nights," Kai said. "I think it rests when it wants, underground. But either way, I usually stay off the sand when it gets dark. We are at enough of a disadvantage during the day."

Neena nodded gravely. With the decision made, she dug into her bag again, fishing for her blankets. Despite her reservations about Kai—about *everything*—they needed to stay warm.

"If we are staying, you'll need this," she said, handing him one of the blankets.

"Thanks," Kai said appreciatively. She heard him drape it over himself in the dark.

"Where have you slept?" she whispered.

"Sometimes in caves like the one in which we are in," Kai said. "A few times, I found a small patch of rocks between which to tuck myself. I don't sleep much. Each time I close my eyes, I fear I will not awaken."

"Have you built fires?"

Kai shook his head. "I'm afraid the crackling will draw it. It might be an irrational fear, but it has kept me alive. And it is hard to find wood, of course. I keep praying it will lose interest in me. So far, that hasn't happened."

And now, it had an interest in Neena, too. She shuddered as she thought of that.

She couldn't imagine sleeping, knowing the creature was out there. On a normal night, Neena slept fitfully. Most nights, she woke at every noise, ready to defend herself. The fires she lit warded off some of the animals, but more than once, she'd fended off some desperate, hungry predator.

"The sandstorm will help us," Kai repeated, as he shifted in the dark, sounding as if he was trying to convince himself.

A rumble preceded another flash. In the bright light, she saw Kai holding a finger to his lips, making it clear that they should return to silence. She studied his face, wondering if she would have to fend him off, too.

Kai had saved her from the beast.

He'd pushed her to the ground before she was devoured.

Neena couldn't forget that.

And yet, she was still uneasy. For now, she had no choice but to trust the strange man with whom she was trapped. Holding her knife tight in her hands, she traded her focus between the cave's entrance and the strange man next to her, knowing they were both in for a sleepless night.

Chapter 12: Raj

WHEN RAJ OPENED HIS EYES, a thin haze of dust hung over the room, sneaking underneath the threshold, filtering through whatever small crevices it could find. He cleared off his sand-splattered goggles and did a slow inspection of the room.

"Is it over?" Samel whispered, still huddling close.

"I think so," Raj answered, blinking hard at his brother.

He said a silent prayer, thanking the heavens that the roof and walls had held.

"Do you think everyone's all right?" Samel asked.

Raj paused a moment, listening for voices outside, hearing a few echoes between the walls of the neighboring houses.

"I hope," Raj said. "We need to find Helgid. She's probably worried about us."

Raj slowly got to his feet, stretching his cramped legs. He walked to the doorway, with Samel behind. Looking over at his brother, he verified he was unharmed. The story of that young boy came back to him, as he recalled the child buried beneath the wreckage of the storm, but Samel seemed fine. He looked like a strange insect in his shawl and goggles. If the situation were different, Raj might've laughed. Reaching the door, they paused.

More voices came from outside as people emerged.

"Keep your face covered," Raj said.

Samel nodded as Raj opened the door to daylight.

Memories of the fitful night's sleep came back to him. Each time he'd felt sleep coming, some new screech of the wind had ripped him awake, or the pelting debris on the roof made him fear it would collapse. He blinked his tired eyes under the light of a new day.

A thicker mist of sand permeated the air, transforming the houses around them into silhouettes. The sand between the mud brick houses was higher next to the dwellings' walls, as if the storm was a strange creature, trying to scale the stone. A few of the scarce, green weeds that grew between the homes had been torn up and cast aside. Pieces of stray fabric stuck in the branches of the scant few trees that occupied the colony, not yet burned for wood. A piece of a pot that must've been left out was partially buried, poking up from the landscape.

Hearing the creak of a door, Raj looked over at his neighbor's house. A young woman stared through the threshold, fixing the goggles on her head.

"Are you okay?" Raj called to the woman.

She nodded.

More and more people emerged from their houses, craning their necks and peering cautiously about. Children hugged their parents' waists, inching out nervously. Some of the elderly opened their doors just wide enough to glimpse the outside, as if the raging sand might return and carry them off. A few of the earliest—and bravest—of the colonists were already sweeping off debris and assessing the damage to their homes. Raj saw a few holes in some of those dwellings' walls, where the fierce storm had torn a new opening.

A sandstorm was always a harsh, powerful lesson.

Raj said, "We should look for anyone else who might need help."

"Dad always said that, didn't he?" Samel asked.

"Yes," Raj repeated.

Raj doubted Samel had many firm recollections of their father. His little brother had only been four when Pradeep left.

"Dad was a good person, wasn't he?" Samel asked.

"Of course he was," Raj said. "Why do you ask?"

Samel looked as if he was working on a troubling thought. "Those kids said he left because of us."

Raj bit back the anger the storm made him forget. "You know that's not true."

"Are you sure?" Samel looked over at him.

"Dad left because he got sick," Raj said. "He did it for our own good."

"I know it is the honorable thing, but I can't understand why," Samel said, confusion crossing his face, as it always did.

Trying to keep the sadness out of his voice, Raj said, "We didn't have a lot of food. He didn't want us to have to take care of him. He wasn't going to survive the sickness, and he didn't want us to catch it." He watched Samel's curious face as he processed it. "That is what the noblest people do, so their families can eat."

"Couldn't the healers have saved him?" Samel asked.

"He was beyond that," Raj said. "Everyone knew it."

"I wish he was here. And I wish Mom hadn't died, so I could've met her."

"So do I. But we have Neena and Helgid," Raj said. "And we have each other."

"I guess you're right."

Raj swallowed the lump in his throat. In the beginning days after their father's departure, the neighbors had helped, but eventually the free meals had ended. Nobody could afford to feed another family when they could barely take care of their own. Neena's hunting sustained them, and Raj did his best to stretch the Green Crops they received from The Heads of Colony. That was all they could do.

"Come on, let's get to Helgid's."

They walked past some of their neighbors, calling out to verify they were all right. A few seemed relieved to see them. Others cursed the storm that had given them a pile of work to do. Cutting down a perpendicular alley, they passed a home with several holes in the side. A group of people circled around somebody near the entrance. Creeping closer, Raj saw a boy his age spitting out sand.

"Is he okay?" Raj asked the boy's parents with concern.

"He's fine," said the boy's father. "He got caught underneath a piece of the roof when it fell. He lost his shawl. Thank you for asking."

Raj nodded and tugged Samel's hand. "Come on."

A few people acknowledged them with commiserating glances. Others were too preoccupied with checking their loved ones, or tending their houses to notice a few parentless boys. Raj and Samel wound through several more homes, watching a few people clean off the cracked places in their roofs, or walls, getting ready for a long day's work of patching. They had just passed a family, brushing off their door, when Raj heard screams.

A creeping fear skittered through his stomach.

"What's going on?" Samel asked.

"I'm not sure."

Raj pulled his brother through the dust-filled pathways toward the noise, struck with the sudden, terrible premonition that Helgid might be in danger. But the noise was coming from another direction.

"This way, Samel!" Raj called, leading his brother east and toward it.

They followed the shrill cries until they found a house with a thick cloud of dust around it. The roof had caved, creating a large barricade of mud brick in the center. Down each of the structure's sides, small, recessed gaps remained. Raj could see nothing in those dark, rubble-strewn holes.

A young woman knelt at one of the recesses, digging frantically.

"Help!" she screamed, removing a large chunk of brick and casting it aside. "My grandmother's inside!"

"Where?"

"I'm not sure! I can't find her!"

"Stay there, Sam!" Raj called.

His heart slammed against his ribcage as he knelt down on the left-hand side of the dwelling, pulling away some broken bricks, creating a hole he could worm into. Rubble scraped his knees. Sharp rock tore at his hands. Panic hit harder as Raj kept digging, finding something hard that wasn't a brick. After a few more tugs and some digging, he pulled out a dented pot and set it aside. His heart pumped. The debris was everywhere, and it was more than he could clear himself.

He could already hear others' voices, drawn toward the commotion, but he didn't stop.

Raj pulled away sand and stone, uncovering several pieces of cookware, another blanket, and some rags. Underneath the shadow of the collapsed ceiling, Raj felt as if he was in some deep, dark cave. From the other side of the building, he heard the frantic young woman crying as she searched.

Raj's hands met something soft.

A hand.

"I found her!" he screamed over his shoulder.

Frantic, he tried pulling, but there was no way he was getting an adult from beneath a pile of fallen stone. He squeezed the person's fingers, hoping for a response, but the person was lifeless, still. Raj dug at the sand around the body, hopelessly trying to free the person.

Shouts echoed behind him.

A group of people crawled in behind him, barking commands and lifting bricks.

"We've got it!" someone yelled, patting Raj's shoulder and taking over.

Raj backed up and scooted outside, allowing the people access. A growing crowd appeared. More people hovered around the broken house and the opening Raj had created. Some people jumped in to help, while others shook their heads, or held their hands over their shawl-covered mouths. A few parents shielded their children's eyes. Raj looked for Samel, finding him in a cluster of others, wringing his hands. Raj hurried to him and held him close.

After more digging, the rescuers pulled a sand-covered body from beneath the rubble, carrying it out. Raj watched as the rescuers dusted off a person's face, body, and clothes.

An old woman stared blankly at the sky.

"Do something!" the frantic young woman screamed to the rescuers.

The people bent over the body, yelling, wiping the dirt away and asking if the woman was all right. Wispy gray hair framed her dusted, ashen face. Her mouth was agape, filled with sand.

Eventually, the people helping wrung their hands, and someone made a pronouncement.

"She's dead."

Raj pulled Samel tighter.

Chapter 13: Darius

ARIUS WALKED THROUGH THE DEBRIS piled between
the sand swept homes. Everywhere he looked, men
and women cleaned sand from their mud brick
dwellings. The hovels were a blessing during storms such
as these, but in other ways, they were prisons, cooping up
the colonists until the storm ended. With the storm raging,
it was easy to fear that the chaos would never end, and
they would be trapped forever. He looked up at one of the
looming, red silhouettes in the distance.

The details of his nightmare came rushing back to him.
Darius blinked hard, casting them back into the recesses of
his memory.

Back in the alleys, every door was open, and every
colonist was outside, looking things over, or checking on
one another. Several picked up pieces of mud brick that had
come from their roofs or walls. The houses on the colony's
western side had stood for many years, proving their worth
in the face of too many storms, but this storm had been
severe.

Luckily, Darius's house had held.

He limped on with his cane, passing several of his
neighbors. All of them had the same sobering expression
that came with each storm. Their grave expressions would
last until the effects of the storm had passed.

With a storm this bad, it was a slim hope there were no
casualties.

Soon, The Heads of Colony would be out with their assessments and their stern faces. After each storm, they made their rounds, determining the damage and the deaths. Once they knew the impact, they assigned able-bodied colonists to help those in need. Even if he had damage, Darius would refuse their help. He wouldn't take assistance away from those who might need it more.

In the general area of his home, a few people checked on him, noticing him hobbling past, but no one stopped to converse. They knew him as the old man who fixed their spears and knives, nothing more. They had families — and problems — of their own.

Darius sometimes felt as if he were a ghost, drifting past the people around him. If not for the rhythmic thud of his cane, he might've convinced himself he was invisible. Looking at some of the people and their families, it was easy to feel that way.

Darius had never married. Most of his younger years had been spent sneaking into the caves, looking for treasures leftover from the first colonists. He had become an expert on maneuvering through those dank tunnels, finding the animals that lurked there, and bringing them back for food. His parents' scolding hadn't gone far with Darius. Each time he agreed to stay away from the formations, he ended up returning.

Everyone feared the punishments of The Heads of Colony.

Everyone except Darius.

His accident changed that.

When Darius was twenty-five years old, he'd been scavenging along a narrow ledge in a tunnel's bowels when a bat dove at his head, knocking him off balance. Darius had grabbed for a handhold, but found nothing. After falling many feet, he'd landed hard, fracturing a bone in his right leg. Despite tremendous pain, Darius had crawled for most of a day to get out of the caves, finding his way back without a torch, eventually making his way to the sunlight. Darius had lived, but the long journey out of the caves had worsened the injury, and he had lost the use of his leg.

He still remembered the crowd that had gathered around him that day as he pulled his dirty, bloodied body from the mouth of one of the tunnels.

A few kindly people had sent for a healer.

For several days afterward, The Heads of Colony and The Watchers had questioned him, thinking he was a criminal. More than one had threatened to throw him in the annex for a month, even a year. A few suggested he remain in there forever, for breaking the laws and venturing into the caves. Eventually, they decided his intentions weren't nefarious.

Or perhaps they decided that the loss of his shattered leg was punishment enough.

Overnight, Darius went from a respected person in Red Rock to a warning parents used to frighten their children. His accident ruined any chance he had at securing a woman to marry — no woman wanted a crippled man. Most turned away from Darius, and in turn, he withdrew, spending most of his time indoors, fixing things for those few colonists kind enough to give him work.

Now he was an old man, whose stories had mostly been forgotten.

But he'd never forget Akron.

Darius still remembered the day when Akron's parents had sent him to Darius's house to ask him to fix a spear. Unlike most of the colonists, who only spoke to Darius long enough to give him instructions, or exchange surface pleasantries, Akron had taken a keen interest in his work, hanging around as he made the repair. Darius had told him stories of the caves, describing each of the places where he'd found some of his scavenged metal — remnants from the miners — or in the case of a few older keepsakes that he'd hung on to, where his father and grandfather had found them in the desert.

Akron kept returning long after the spear was fixed.

Eventually, Darius came to enjoy his visits, and Akron turned from an acquaintance to a friend.

If Darius could have foreseen how his stories would spark a passion in the boy, he would've never told them. Looking up at the silhouette of the enormous, red rock formation on the colony's eastern side, where Darius suspected he'd disappeared, he felt the same pit in his stomach he did with every sandstorm.

It was his fault Akron had journeyed to the caves on that day, like he had done so many other days. And in an indirect way, it was Darius's fault he had died.

Chapter 14: Gideon

G IDEON WALKED AMONG A PILE of sand and wreckage, assessing one of the collapsed homes. Around the outside walls, and inside, a family worked to clear the fallen stones. The woman's crushed body had already been covered with a blanket. Tear streaks marked only the youngest faces, those who were too busy mourning to realize that a hard day's work was the quickest way to ease their grief.

"How many other deaths?" Gideon asked Wyatt.

"Two in another house to the north." Wyatt stared curiously at the family as he watched them work. His face was strangely thoughtful, as he rubbed his bony cheeks, probably calculating numbers and tallying the impact on the population.

"Anyone of consequence?"

"A man and a woman," Wyatt said. "Tenders of the Green Crops."

"A shame," Gideon said. It always hurt to lose such knowledge.

Pointing to the body under the blanket, another of The Heads of Colony, Brody, said, "This was an older woman, named Joan, I believe."

Gideon nodded gravely. There were too many names in Gideon's colony to know them all. Tomorrow morning, when most of the dust had cleared and the shock of the deaths had worn off, he would say some words to comfort his people while they performed a group burial. But for now, his concentration was on assessment and rebuilding.

It was unlikely another sandstorm would hit in rapid succession, but they needed to be prepared.

Behind him, Saurab and Horatio looked over the houses to the left and right, perhaps searching for flaws in the structure that would lead to damage in subsequent storms. Finishing their assessment, they continued on south, toward the river and the crops.

Walking through the dusty village, Gideon thought of that first generation, scrapping it out on the ratty weeds they could find on a mostly barren planet while they built the first homes in the colony, or hunted animals whose habits they were still learning. In a way, his people had it better. They were more realistic. Most lived without the foolish hope that a ship from the stars would rescue them, or that some higher power would take pity on them and perform a miracle, like the miracles for which their ancestors had prayed. Most accepted there were no secret resources to find on the planet, like the first generation thought when they'd first colonized and explored. And they certainly had less vicious predators to face. Ravar was, for the most part, a harsh desert environment where only the scrappiest animals survived.

From what Gideon had heard — recounted by his father, passed from his grandfather, and some people before that — it had taken several years for their ancestors to accept they'd been abandoned. During the first year, supply ships would land regularly, checking on the colonists who sought out things of value. Their food stores and water supply were supplemented to ensure their survival. In the event the storms were too severe, the plan was to pull out the colonists.

Soon, the supply ships stopped landing.

Contact was lost.

Frantic, the first generation had sent messages to Earth

on strange metal contraptions, asking for assistance, but those signals were never answered. Eventually, dwindling resources and severe storms forced the colonists to build more permanent shelter. That's when they'd doubled down between the twin, parallel formations they'd called Red Rock. Looming high above the river, the cliffs provided a place of shelter from some of the high winds and storms, and provided a place between which to build their permanent homes. Each time a severe storm struck the colony, Gideon thought of those first, temporary dwellings, and how much worse the casualties could have been.

Three casualties was not a large toll.

Even with the protection of the mud brick houses, Gideon wasn't blind to the challenges.

The crops were dwindling, and the animals were harder to find. More and more families subsisted on less and less. That was one of the reasons he had instituted a new law about the number of children in a family, and the rations to be taken from the crops. He had limited hunting to certain areas, those that were safer, and not too far away.

Control. It was the only way to ensure the survival of his people.

Without order, the colonists would burn themselves to the ground.

He looked behind him, where Wyatt, Brody, Horatio, and Saurab observantly measured the storm's damage. Then he looked up to the cliffs, where his Watchers stood observantly, carrying out his orders.

He had a greater worry than people.

Gideon was more concerned about the loss of crops than the loss of three lives. A shortage could lead to a breakdown of order, which would mean a much greater catastrophe.

Chapter 15: Neena

ORNING SUNLIGHT FOUND ITS WAY through the cave's hazy entrance.

Neena sat up, blinking twice to ensure she was awake. What little dozing she'd done was filled with dreams of a looming, massive beast coming from the ground, devouring her. More than once, she had peered through the darkness in Kai's direction, thinking he might change his nature and come for her.

He hadn't.

She adjusted her goggles as spears of daylight illuminated her surroundings. Kai sat a few feet away, clutching his knees, breathing softly. He met her eyes.

Neither of them dared speaking.

Their look said it all.

We're alive.

Slowly, they crawled over to the cave's entrance. A small bed of sand and sticks was spread across the opening, creating an uneven platform near the cave's entrance. Reaching it, they stopped, as if an invisible line stood between them and the outside. Neena looked beyond. A few, scarce weeds around the cave's entrance were bent over and crusted with sand. Some small rocks around the cave's entrance had broken, fallen, and cracked at the threshold.

The desert was covered in a dusty cloud. The silhouettes of the dunes were flattened, or reshaped. Light emanated from high up in the sky, in the direction of the sun and the twin moons.

She saw no monster.

No jagged, waiting teeth.

With the sun piercing through the dust, and the wind gone, it would be easy to think they were safe, if she didn't know better. If the beast was out there, they might be dead as soon as they took a step outside.

Kai surveyed the landscape with the same trepidation. The three markings on either side of his hairline seemed even darker in the daytime. The dark, heavy bags under his eyes showed he hadn't slept or dozed much, either. After a while of watching, Kai raised an arm and pointed in the distance, on the eastern side of one of the flattened dunes, where the sun shone through the dusty landscape.

Leaning close enough that Neena could smell his nervous sweat, he hissed, "Do you see that?"

Neena squinted, spotting what had gotten his attention. A large, black hole sat in the ground about fifty yards away, and another fifty yards north.

"It surfaced, looking for us," he whispered.

"Is it gone?"

Kai shook his head. Of course, he didn't know. Slowly, he dragged a hand across his dry, cracked lips. He must be as parched as she was. Neena removed one of her two flasks and handed it over.

"We're running low on water," she warned.

Kai sipped modestly. After a small drink, he said, "Several times, I thought I heard it in the night, and thought we might have to run."

Neena nodded. She had thought the same thing, even though the cave was supposed to protect them. She recalled what Kai had told her the night before. *I can't promise our safety.*

A scuttling noise ripped their attention behind.

Neena spun.

She thrust out her knife.

Her eyes flitted from floor to ceiling, as she waited for the ground to shake, or something to crash through a wall.

A sand rat sat in the middle of the rocky floor, staring at them with unblinking eyes.

It watched them a moment, before scurrying off and burrowing in a crevice in the cave's wall. Neena lowered her knife with relief.

"That's a good sign," Kai said, at a more normal volume.

"What do you mean?" Neena asked.

"The animals won't come out if the creature is close. It is something I've learned, in my time being chased," he said, scratching the stubble on his chin. "The creatures in the desert are as afraid of the Abomination as we are. They sense the rumbling underground, before we hear it. Or at least, that's what I think."

A recollection hit Neena, as she thought back to the moments preceding the frantic chase. "The Rydeer knew the beast was coming."

Kai nodded. "The animals have other instincts we do not have. In any case, their fear is a good indicator of when it is close." He took another small sip of her flask, before handing it back. With his pronouncement made, Kai stood, stretching his legs. He seemed cautious, but a little less anxious.

"Yesterday, you knocked me to the ground," Neena remembered, finally voicing her appreciation. "You saved me, before the creature could eat me."

"And you saved my life, by giving me water," Kai said honestly. "But if the Abomination catches us, neither of those things will matter."

"The Abomination," she repeated, pronouncing the word the same way he had. "What is it?"

"No one knows for sure, but it has plagued our colony for as long as I can remember." Kai quietly brushed off his clothes. "If the stories are to be believed, it has existed for generations, feeding on our people, mostly in the desert."

"Where did it come from?"

"No one knows that, either," Kai said.

Neena's eyes grew wide. "I still can't believe my people wouldn't know about it."

Kai shook his head. "Maybe it lives far enough away that you've never seen it. In any case, you are fortunate."

The questions that had plagued Neena the night before came tumbling back into her head. "You said New Canaan is far from here, or at least you suspect that it is. Are you alone?"

Kai looked at the ground. "I wish I was with others. The rest of my hunting party is dead."

"Dead?" Neena couldn't hide her shock.

"I'm the last of my group." Sadness crossed Kai's face as he looked from Neena out into the desert, to the two murky holes. "The Abomination killed the hunters I was with."

Dread filled her stomach. "How many died?"

"Ten."

Neena shook her head. "And you're certain they're dead?"

"I'm certain." Kai lowered his head. "I heard the screams. I saw the creature swallow them whole, as it erupted from the ground. Its massive body crushed those who weren't eaten. The wake of sand threw me to the side, or I would've been killed or eaten, too." A wave of emotion hit Kai as he lifted his goggles and dabbed at his eyes. "Everyone I traveled with is gone."

"I'm sorry," Neena said, feeling a wave of empathy that she hadn't anticipated.

Kai shook his head in grief. "I knew most of those hunters for years. We grew up together. It is difficult thinking about their loss." With a long sigh, he explained, "We were a few days away from my colony when it happened. One of us had shot a Rydeer, but the shot wasn't fatal, and we were following it while it bled out. A few of us were moving quickly, hoping we didn't lose sight of it. We must've made too much noise. The creature's rumbles came up so loud and fast that we didn't have much time to react. I was thrown to the ground when it erupted. My bag went one way, and my spear, the other. In my haste to get away, I had no time to retrieve my belongings. I suspect that most of my gear was buried, or fell down the holes, but I'll never know, because I didn't go back." Kai shook his head at the memory. "I ran as far and as fast as I could. My instinctive response almost killed me, because the creature followed my vibrations, tracking me across the desert. Eventually, I stumbled upon a cave and stayed there for almost a day."

"By the stars." Neena shook her head.

Kai shook his head as he relived that panicked time. "In the cave, I had no water, or a way to collect it. My flasks were with my bag. I was on the verge of dehydration. But I feared going back to New Canaan, knowing that was the direction that I'd last seen the creature. Eventually, my thirst drove me to move. And so, I continued south, hoping to lose it."

"For a while, I had luck walking softly, moving from cave to cave, but the creature was never far behind. When the sandstorm hit, I took the opportunity to move faster, using the noise to cover my travels. I intended to circle back to my colony. That's when I lost direction. I trekked for a while in the storm, hoping to gain enough ground to be rid of it. But it found me. It found *us*." Kai looked down, ashamed. "And now we are both in danger."

"How far away is your colony?"

"I have no idea anymore, because I have no idea where I ended up." Kai looked around, confused.

They stood in silence for a moment, scanning the desert. Kai lowered his head, clearly feeling the loss of his fellow hunters, and still confused. Neena felt a commiserating pit in her stomach. She knew the pain of losing people. Clipping her flask onto her belt, she stood and looked out across the desert.

After a long, sad silence, Kai said, "I wish I could bring back my friends, but, of course, that is impossible."

"I am sorry you lost them."

After a few more moments, he turned to look at her. One of a dozen questions flickered through his eyes as he pushed past his sadness. "Where are you from?"

Neena hesitated. Since the night before, she hadn't revealed more than a few things about herself. She watched Kai for a moment, thinking of the warnings her father gave her when he realized he was dying and she would be alone. Neena knew better than to trust blindly. And yet, she had spent a night alone with this strange man, and he had not attacked her. He had saved her from the creature when he didn't have to. And he had clearly lost some of his people.

"My colony is called Red Rock." She looked for recognition in his face, but saw none.

Sensing her caution, he softened his tone. "If you do not want to tell me too much, I will not pressure you. I'm sure you are careful, as my people are."

"I was out hunting, as you guessed."

"Alone?" he assumed.

Her eyes flicked over the desert. Of course, he probably knew the truth. "Yes."

Kai scanned the desert, where a few birds soared past. "How far away is your colony?"

"Three days," Neena answered.

"Three days," he repeated. "Not close, in other words."

Neena shook her head, wishing she had another answer. "Unfortunately, not. But it sounds as if your colony might be farther."

"Even if I wanted to go back, I have no idea which direction to go," Kai said.

"What do we do now?"

"If we stay here, it will come back for us," Kai said, knowingly.

Looking out into the desert, Neena couldn't imagine taking a step outside the cave. At the very least, she wasn't ready to make a hasty decision. "You said that it has followed you for days, always finding you. Maybe if we wait longer, we will lose it."

"If we stay, we will die," Kai reiterated.

Confusion struck Neena. "What do you mean?"

"When I stayed in that first cave, I made another mistake," Kai explained. "I waited too long for it to leave, and I nearly died of dehydration." His face took on a new level of concern, as he looked at her flasks. "Unless you have water that I am not seeing, we will need more."

Neena nodded. All she had in her bag was a little sand rat, some blankets, and game pouches. Kai was right.

"Is there anything to drink nearby?" Kai asked.

Neena shook her head. "Not here."

"Where is the closest water source?"

"A large rock formation a few klicks away," Neena replied, thinking, but not saying, that was also the direction of her colony. "There's a stream that runs next to it."

"Perhaps we can head for the stream. At the very least, we will be moving further away from the holes, and where we last saw the creature." Kai shrugged. "If we hear rumbling, we can come back. It is all I can think to do."

Neena looked out at the desert for a long moment. Kai was right. They hadn't heard the creature in a while. And they wouldn't last more than a day in the desert without water.

She didn't like the idea of stepping back outside, but at least heading for the stream was a plan.

Chapter 16: Raj

RAJ AND SAMEL HURRIED THROUGH the alleys. Raj would never forget the old, sand-covered woman he'd helped pull from the rubble: her vacant eyes, staring at the heavens, her lifeless fingers clutching at nothing. A growing fear told Raj that he'd find Helgid buried in a layer of wreckage and sand, or a group of people hovering around her body. Helgid wasn't feeble, but the storm didn't discriminate. What if her house had collapsed, too?

Skirting between two houses, he watched some people comforting an older, frightened man. The elderly man smeared sand from his nose, looking disoriented and confused. Seeing the rattled man deepened Raj's fear.

He kept running until his lungs and legs hurt. Samel sucked in rapid breaths, barely keeping up with shorter strides.

Neither slowed until they reached a familiar alley.

Helgid's dwelling was little more than an outline in the encircling haze, but it looked intact. Raj wasn't ready to believe his eyes until he found her. He and Samel raced the last few-dozen steps to the threshold, frantically looking around.

No rubble.

No grieving, circling people.

A good sign, he hoped.

Raj didn't bother knocking. He opened the door, keeping Samel behind with a protective arm.

A few, small holes seemed to be the only damage. The holes made spears of dusty light that shone from the wall to the floor, filling the dwelling with the same dusty cloud that occupied the alleys. Piles of tied-up belongings sat in sheets near the walls. Helgid had heard the horn and reacted.

But what if she'd gone out, right after the storm started? *What if she went looking for us?*

Raj didn't voice his thoughts to Samel, who was already frightened.

"Come on, Samel. Let's check with the neighbors."

Leaving the hovel, they spotted a middle-aged man with a shock of black hair named Amos, one of Helgid's neighbors. Raj hurried toward him, about to voice the question on the tip of his tongue, when someone called his name.

"Raj!"

He and Samel spun.

A figure strode quickly down the alley about thirty feet away, cutting through the dust. Despite the obscuring conditions and her shawl and goggles, Helgid's gait was unmistakable. Raj and Samel changed course, running to meet her.

Raj opened his arms and embraced her, flooded with relief. He and Samel hugged her for several moments, as if she might disappear.

Stepping back, Helgid appraised them, with the same concern on her face that they certainly wore. Long, gray hair poked out of the sides of her shawl. Her brown eyes shone underneath her goggles.

"You're okay," Helgid whispered.

"We were worried about you," Samel said.

"I'm fine." Helgid's eyes creased as she smiled beneath her goggles. "It will take more than a sandstorm to bury me."

"We tried coming back last night," Raj explained. "The storm got too bad, too quickly."

"I know. I started for your house, but Amos said he saw

you run home. He urged me back inside." Helgid looked as if she was still processing her relief.

"I'm just glad you're safe," Raj told her.

Helgid urged them toward the threshold of her dwelling. "Come on. Let's get inside and out of so much dust."

After brushing off their clothes, they walked inside the house. Samel spilled the details of their journey, telling of the collapsed house and the buried woman, and Raj's attempts to dig her out. He told of the crowds of people, helping to unbury the woman, and her wailing, frightened granddaughter. Helgid listened with a grim expression.

"You are brave for what you did," Helgid told Raj, dusting more sand from his shoulders.

Raj swallowed, but he didn't say anything. What did bravery matter, when someone was dead?

Seeing the anxious expression in his eyes, Helgid asked, "What's wrong?"

"I feel bad for the woman's family, that's all." Raj lowered his head.

"Of course, you do." Helgid patted his shoulders. "But you did what you could. You helped her, before others came. That means something."

Raj nodded. Her words reminded him of what Dad might have said, if he had been around. He surveyed Helgid's kind, weathered face. He had only known her for two years, but it felt as if he had known her his whole life. Raj had been eight when he met her. Samel had been four.

It was the first time Neena had gone hunting since their father left, and most of the charity from the neighbors had run out. One of the close neighbors—a mother named Irma—was supposed to be looking out for Raj and Samel, but her hands were full with her own children. And so, they went to the river by themselves, assuring her that they would be all right. Helgid had been with a circle of elderly women, chatting, when she saw Raj and Samel struggling with two buckets of water.

At the time, she was a stranger.

Without a word, Helgid broke from her friends and helped them. Afterward, she invited them to her house for a meal, sharing her meager rations.

What started as a neighborly gesture became a familial bond.

Helgid cared for them as if they were her grandchildren, and Raj felt for her as if she were a grandmother. Sometimes Raj suspected that the only reason Helgid asked for help with chores was so that she had an excuse to feed them.

Pointing at the holes that he had seen in the wall, Raj said, "You have some damage."

"Not too much. Perhaps you can help me patch them," Helgid said, smiling. She took the pieces of broken mud brick on the floor and collected them, temporarily plugging the small openings.

With Helgid safe, Raj's thoughts wandered to his sister. "Have you seen Neena?"

"No." Helgid noticed his expression. "But your sister is savvy. She'll be back soon."

Raj wanted to believe that. Still, he felt an anxiety in his chest. He wanted to wander to the edge of the colony and survey the desert. His uneasiness compelled him to move.

Sensing his thoughts, Helgid said, "Watching the desert for her won't bring Neena home any sooner."

Raj nodded, even though he was still worried.

"When was the last time you two ate?" Helgid asked.

Raj struggled to remember. In Raj and Samel's frantic rush from the river the night before, dinner hadn't crossed their minds. They'd been too preoccupied with surviving the storm.

"I'm going to fix you something," Helgid insisted. "And you should drink plenty of fluid, too."

Raj knew better than to argue with Helgid, who could be as persuasive as she was kind. He reached for his flask and sipped. Samel looked as if he was winding down from some of his anxiety. Another memory came back to Raj. In the frenzy of the storm, they'd both forgotten about Bailey's intimidating threat.

Watching Helgid preparing them supper, Raj decided against saying anything. The last thing she needed was another worry.

Chapter 17: Neena

NEENA DUCKED UNDERNEATH THE CAVE'S protective opening.

Fear froze her feet.

She looked down at the sand, as if a creature might burst through the ground beneath her, crunching her bones, or worse, swallowing her alive. Working through her fear, she lifted a boot, took a furtive step, and then another, getting farther away from the cave. Kai followed quietly.

The heat of the desert day baked through the dusty sand clouds, creating a glare off their goggles. Without the shrieking wind, the desert felt unnaturally calm. Neena clutched her knife as she looked over at the giant, gaping holes, which slanted north. Despite the apparent clue, they had no idea where the creature headed now.

"Stay away from the holes," Kai warned, making sure to keep a wide berth around the cave-sized openings.

"Is there anything else in them?" Neena asked.

"Besides sand?" Kai asked. "I don't know. And I don't want to."

Neena nodded. She didn't need him to tell her twice.

They fell into a rhythm next to each other, walking as if they were on a hunt, looking over their shoulders, or scanning the horizon, looking for evidence of the creature. Several times, Neena thought she heard noises, but each time, it proved to be a hungry bird squawking overhead, or an occasional, brave sand rat scuttling past. She felt a degree safer with the animals around, but not safe enough.

"Remember what I said," Kai said quietly. "If we hear rumbles, don't panic, like I did. Running is an easy way to death. It makes our vibrations more noticeable."

Neena agreed, until a memory came back to her. "Yesterday, when you first met me, we ran. Was that because of the sandstorm?"

"Partially, yes. But there was another reason. With the creature so close and surfacing, it might've crushed us, like it did to some of my comrades. It was a last resort." Kai said gravely. "Normally, if we hear the rumbles, we should stay still. Or if we are near a cave, we should get to it."

Thinking of the creature's enormous, scaled body, Neena realized most of its appearance had been a blur. She hadn't seen much more than its girth, its grinding teeth, and its gaping maw. "Does the Abomination have eyes?" she asked, feeling a shudder of fear as she spoke of it by name.

"I don't think so," Kai said. "I think it is blind, like the earthworms in the soil. But it senses light and dark, somehow, because it stays underground. It hunts us by vibrations. Then it surfaces and eats."

Neena nodded. "So, the only way to avoid it is to look for caves?"

"It's what I've been doing." Kai fell silent as he thought about something. "Although I can't guarantee that it will work forever." He chewed his lip. "The Abomination is a force of nature. It eats, and it kills. It feeds its stomach. We might as well be sand rats to it. I think it will do what it needs for a meal."

A shimmer of fear went through Neena's body. Thinking of those strange, jagged spears she'd glimpsed on its body, she asked, "What were those things on its sides?"

"Quills?"

"Is that what you call them?"

"Some say those spear-like things help it tunnel through the ground," Kai explained. "Others say they are for protection, when larger creatures are around. Of course, no one has seen anything close to its size. I think the Abomination is the last of its kind. Our people haven't been able to pierce its hide with spears or arrows. We've tried many things over the years, but none of them worked."

Neena envisioned the beast's monstrous body and its jagged, bloodstained teeth. Of course, it was much too large for any weapons she knew.

"Thankfully, it seems to prefer the desert, or at least, that is where we most often run into it." Kai thought on that. "But a few times recently, it has gotten bolder, and attacked our colony."

"Is your colony on the sand?"

"Our homes are built of firmer soil, but it can get through the ground without a problem. Our people have discussed moving, but that would be a massive undertaking."

"How many people are in your colony?" Neena asked, still processing the existence of another people.

"Three thousand," Kai said. "Our colony is located in an oasis, with plenty of water. We have lived there for as long as I can remember. A few times, some of our leaders have tried leading the creature away, but it always seems to come back. Most of our plans don't work, and people die." Kai shook his head gravely. "If we moved, who is to say it wouldn't find us somewhere else?"

Neena sighed. "Or it might kill you along the way."

Kai nodded. Looking over his shoulder, he said, "In any case, I'm glad you knew of that cave."

Neena followed his gaze, watching the rock formation fade into the haze of dust. The sight of it brought back some buried nostalgia. "I found it with my father, many years ago."

"Is he waiting for you in Red Rock?"

Neena hesitated. "He's dead."

"I'm sorry," Kai said.

If the loss had been fresh, it might've brought tears. Instead, it brought a memory. "I found the cave when I was thirteen years old. We were hunting together," Neena said, her thoughts drifting back to that time. "I was walking by the outside, admiring the smooth rock walls, when I found the opening. I remember my father scolding me as I went through the entrance, saying it wasn't safe. Eventually, he followed me in. When he saw that there was enough room to move around in the cave, he was too impressed to be angry. In all his years, he had never known about it."

"Sometimes it takes new eyes to see new things," Kai said reflectively, looking up at the sky.

"Is that something your people say?"

"My mother did, when I was younger," Kai said, smiling. "She used to enjoy watching me react to things for the first time. My wonder made her smile, or so she said."

"She sounds like a kind person," Neena said. "Is your father around, too?"

"He is, but we don't get along." Kai shrugged. "But that happens sometimes with parents. They are both at my colony."

"I understand," Neena said. "My dad taught me everything he knew about hunting, before he died. I think he did it so that I could take care of my brothers. Sometimes, I feel as if he knew he wouldn't be around for long, though I don't know how that could be true. My mother died giving birth to my youngest brother. After Dad died, we were alone."

Gently, making it clear that he wouldn't push, Kai asked, "What happened to him?"

"A few years ago, he came down with a sickness that took the weight from his bones," Neena explained. "He grew so tired that normal tasks were a struggle. When he could no longer hunt, he left for the desert in the night, so that my brothers and I would not have to feed him. He left his spear behind for me."

"He left you?" Kai asked, surprised.

Neena nodded. "As most of our people do, when they are gravely ill. It is the honorable thing to do."

Kai seemed confused.

"It sounds as if your people do not have the same tradition."

Kai shook his head, but he didn't judge her. "That is not the way of our colony, but I am sure we have many differences." Moving on from a sad subject, he asked, "You have two brothers?"

"Yes. They are named Raj and Samel. I have to get back to them. I am supposed to bring back food. I am all they have."

"Do you have a husband in Red Rock? Children?"

Neena shook her head. "Just them."

Kai nodded. "It sounds as if you are a good sister."

"I do what I need," Neena said simply.

They fell silent for a while as they kept walking. Neena listened for rumbles, or the screech of fleeing animals — anything that would signify a tunneling creature. She heard or saw nothing as the sun rose higher into the sky, cutting through the dust left over from the storm.

Over the course of the morning, the haze lifted from the landscape, revealing a plethora of flattened dunes. A light breeze scattered some of the sand around their bases. More than once, Neena looked up at the sky, confirming their direction of travel.

The planet she'd known all her life seemed foreign, strange, as if the storm had lifted her up and displaced her. She couldn't be certain she wasn't living some waking dream. Kai's presence added to the journey's abnormality. Still, it felt good to have someone around who knew something about the monster, even though she wasn't ready to give him her complete trust.

They traveled for half a day under the hot rays of the sun, skirting around endless mounds of leveled sand, until a building hunger in Neena's stomach became too difficult to ignore.

"Are you hungry?" she asked quietly, removing her pack.

Kai nodded, wiping away some sweat from his brow.

Neena dug in her bag, pulling out the last of her dried sand rat. "Here," she said, splitting it.

Kai received the food gratefully, lowering his shawl to eat. Neena chewed mindlessly.

"I think this is the best sand rat I've tasted in years," Kai said with a grave smile. "In any case, it is much better than scraproot. How much food do you have left?"

"That was the last of it," Neena said.

Guilt crossed Kai's face. "I did not mean to take the last of your rations."

"If we survive, you can pay me back," she said, smiling grimly. "Or maybe we can find a safe place to trap some more."

Finishing the last of his food, Kai said, "It sounds as if your colony is as starved as mine."

Neena nodded as she thought about that. "I can't remember a time when food was plentiful. Lots of the creatures we used to hunt seemed to have disappeared. We are lucky to find many Rydeer anymore."

"Even the sand rats seem savvier than they used to be," Kai agreed with a sigh.

"Our ancestors had more creatures from which to choose, but I fear we have eaten too many," Neena said, repeating a theory of which she had heard the old people whisper. Everyone knew about the skulls of the dead animals in the Comm Building. A few had even glimpsed them. As gruesome and frightening as those creatures seemed to have been, it would've been nice to have more sources of food, other than Rydeer, dust beetles, plants, and the elusive wolves that were too dangerous to catch.

With her mind on Red Rock, her thoughts wandered to Raj and Samel. She'd thought of them often, especially during the night, when she thought she might die and never see them again. Having them out of her sight always caused her worry.

Had the sandstorm reached as far as Red Rock?

She wished she knew.

She looked over her shoulder, a habit that became as instinctual as treading lightly. Seeing nothing, Neena allowed a small hope to build: in the time they'd traveled, she hadn't seen any indication of the creature. No fearful rodents. No massive, gaping holes. Maybe they would find the luck that had evaded Kai.

They had just passed a dune when she spotted a tall, thin rock formation in the distance. Neena's hope grew.

"That's the formation of which I spoke," she said, pointing with her knife.

Kai shielded his goggles from the sun's glare as he appraised the tall, auburn spire. The large, craggy formation was about the width of a dozen people lying sideways, rising about a hundred feet in the air. In several places, ledges jutted out from the sides. In others, gaps recessed into the rock, where smaller pieces had broken away and fallen over time. Chunks of rock surrounded its base, leaning up against it, or spaced at various angles and distances. Neena didn't see any animals hiding among them, but she did see a few circling birds.

"Look up there," she said, pointing them out.

"It is good to see them," Kai said with relief.

"The stream is on the western side," she told him, veering in that direction. "It is small and partially hidden by the rocks. I've stayed behind them, during a few, lesser storms."

"Are there any caves here?"

"Unfortunately not," Neena said. "But we can fill our flasks, at least."

That statement put some energy into Kai's steps, propelling him onward. Even the tug of the sand on Neena's boots seemed less arduous. They moved quietly, but quickly, until they got within fifteen feet of the structure.

Neena clutched her knife as they rounded the side of the formation. A jutting overhang protruded at eye level. Several craggy rocks provided shade from the sun. They followed the overhang to the formation's south side, until they glimpsed the small stream, wending out from some lower rocks and curving underneath the structure fifteen feet away.

A few birds alighted from something in the desert.

Neena froze.

Farther out in the desert, a furry mound of flesh baked in the desert heat. Its intestines were chewed and unraveled. Neena covered her mouth as she discerned what the object had been.

The remains of a fawn.

On either side of the fawn's carcass were two enormous, gaping holes.

Chapter 18: Darius

ARIUS WANDERED THROUGH THE BEATEN Red Rock alleys. Most of the pathways were covered in a fresh layer of sand, erasing the tread of the colonists' boots. Those paths, he knew, would soon be beaten down, as more and more people returned to their normal duties and carried out repairs. Earlier, he heard the distant cries of mourning women, but those cries had long since ceased. He prayed that the casualties were few.

Slowly, the fear in the colonists' eyes turned to a bustling determination, as more and more of them flowed past him and to the river, filling up buckets of water and mud to make their patches, or waiting in line for their disbursement of straw. Their children helped, all wrapped in the same shawls and goggles they would wear for most of the day, until the last of the dust had cleared and they could breathe without worry.

Darius pulled his shawl tight against his face. Too much walking and grasping his cane made his fingers ache. Normally, Darius knew his limitations, but sometimes, like today, he had a reason to break them.

He had someone on whom to check.

Adjusting his goggles, he headed east, in the direction of the red rock formations that towered high above the colony, passing a few streams of people. A few nodded curtly.

Eventually, Darius reached a home built a little distance away from the others, on the end of a row. He was relieved to find it intact. The faded, round house had stood since long before Darius was born, and he expected it would survive much longer.

"Elmer?" he called.

Darius blinked, as if that might allow him to see through the remaining haze of sand that encircled the house. He wiped his goggles.

"Elmer?" he called again.

The door stood ajar, but he didn't see movement. A shuffling noise drew his attention to the rear of the house, where a man even older than Darius ambled around a corner, clutching a rusted shovel. Patchy white hair stuck up around the man's weathered face. His face lit up when he saw who visited.

"Is that you?" the older man asked, blinking one blue, cataract-covered eye, struggling to see through the other. A half-smile tugged at Elmer's wrinkles as he confirmed that it was his friend. "Darius! You made it."

"We both did," Darius said with a smile of relief.

Elmer placed an appreciative hand on Darius's shoulder. "It is good to see you, my friend."

"Another day alive is a blessing," Darius said.

Elmer took his hand away, scratching his bristly chin. "How did your house fare?"

"A few cracked bricks," Darius answered. "Nothing I can't manage."

"I keep waiting for the day this old shack goes over," Elmer said, lifting his shovel and pointing at his house. "Maybe by the time it does, I'll be too blind to notice."

Darius smiled. Even on a dreary day, Elmer kept his humor.

"Do you need help clearing the sand?"

"I'll be fine." Elmer waved a hand. "As long as I have sight in one good eye, and the strength to shovel, I'll keep digging."

Darius nodded. He had expected that answer. Elmer was determined, as he was.

"I haven't seen you in a few days," Elmer noticed.

"I've been...busy," Darius said.

"Too many spears to fix?" Elmer asked, making it clear that he wouldn't push for an answer.

For the past few days, Darius's leg had been bothering him. Or maybe it was the memories of Akron, which never seemed far from his thoughts. The sudden sandstorm made those memories even worse. Akron had disappeared in the midst of a similar storm, several years ago.

Elmer smiled sympathetically, probably picking up on Darius's resurfaced pain.

Elmer knew the grief that could sap a man's will, making it hard to step outside of his home. He knew about the despair that lived within a suffering man's heart, making his grief deeper when he saw the honest smiles around him. Years earlier, Elmer had lost his wife to sickness. Ever since, his bond with Darius had strengthened. That wasn't their only commonality. Elmer knew secrets about Darius that a less trustworthy man might use against him.

"I'm glad you're okay," Elmer said, relief evident in his voice.

Darius looked around at the people cleaning their homes. "Have you seen The Heads of Colony?"

"They already came past, assessing the damage," Elmer said. "I overheard them talking. Three people died during the night."

Darius shook his head. "Any idea who?"

"A woman our age to the north, near the front of the colony. I didn't know her." Elmer shook his head. "And a few Crop Tenders, a dozen alleys west."

"It is a shame."

Darius looked around, as if he might catch a glimpse of Gideon and his men, but they were gone. For most of the day, they would direct the clean-up, tally the dead, and oversee the handout of straw, along with their Watchers. Likewise, they would assess the damage to the crops, while the Crop Tenders saved what they could.

"I am sad about the deaths, but the destruction of the crops will make for even hungrier stomachs, which could lead to more casualties," Elmer said.

Darius knew that was true. They might have a surplus for a day or two, but a meal today meant a deficit tomorrow.

Elmer said, "I suppose we will have a ceremony to attend tomorrow morning."

Darius nodded.

"Will I see you there?" Elmer asked.

"Possibly," Darius said. "Depending on how my leg feels."

Elmer nodded, but he didn't ask any more probing questions.

Darius headed in a westerly direction, taking a different route home. A few people looked over, tentatively waving. In one doorway, a mother scolded a child who had exited a dwelling without shutting the door. The child skirted away, avoiding the mother's reprimand. Catching the child's attention, Darius raised his cane and smiled.

He hobbled on.

When he was halfway down the alley, Darius slowed to a stop next to a gap in the houses, close enough that he could see through the clouded next alley. He stuck close to the wall of the closest dwelling, verifying that no one paid him any mind.

Through the alley, he glimpsed the squalid, dilapidated house that he'd come to find. A wave of relief washed over him as he found the house standing. The door was shut. He watched for a while until the door opened and a woman thirty years his junior popped out, holding a shovel. She kept her head down as she walked to a mound of sand on the side of the house, scooping it up and depositing it into a pushcart. Later, Darius knew, she would bring it to a dump area closer to the cliffs, where The Watchers would bring it out into the desert, like they did for the other colonists.

A few moments later, a man joined the woman, clothed in his protective garb. Neither spoke as they did their work. A few neighbors came out from their houses, looking over, but they refrained from speaking to the couple.

Eventually, the man and woman completed their task, and the man wheeled away the unwanted sand. The woman stuck her shovel in the ground, adjusting her shawl. When she finished, she gazed up through the dust clouds.

Slowly, she appraised the outline of the giant, red rock formation that hung in the distance — an enormous, towering reminder of a loss neither she nor Darius would forget.

Darius felt as if someone had punched his stomach. Sadness washed over him as he watched Akron's mother. He wanted to reach out to her, console her, and share his sympathies.

But she hated him, just as her husband did. They blamed him for telling the stories that had inspired Akron to go into the caves, leading to his death.

They were right. It was Darius's fault.

One day, he would give Akron's parents peace.

Darius watched Akron's mother for another moment, until the guilt in his stomach got the better of him and he hobbled along.

Chapter 19: Neena

A SLOW WIND PICKED UP ACROSS the desert, blowing sand over the gaping holes, piling it against the rock formation and covering the bloodied carcass. The sight of the mangled animal and the scavenging birds gave Neena a sickening wave of fear. The holes on either side of the carcass were black, filled with shadow. They were fifty feet apart—spaced a hundred feet from the rock formation. For all she knew, the creature lurked in one of them, ready to rise up and end their lives.

She couldn't be certain the fawn was the same one she'd seen, but deep down, she knew.

First the mother, and now its child.

Overhead, the squawking birds chose a new direction. Were they fleeing Neena, Kai, or something else?

"This way," Kai hissed.

Without another word, he hurried to the stream and filled his flask. Neena followed suit. Right after, he directed her to the nearest jutting overhang, curved his fingers over the top, and pulled himself up and over. She knew what he was doing. Staying on the ground seemed like inviting death.

Following him, Neena heaved herself up the craggy, red rock and climbed. Her breath came in ragged gasps as she grunted and pulled, finding hand and footholds, avoiding slick bird droppings on the steep formation's face, and stones sharp enough to cut her flesh. Several times, she slowed, thinking she might lose her grip, but she held on. The image of the creature's enormous teeth clamping an ankle pushed her faster.

Looking up, she saw where Kai aimed. Twenty feet skyward, a ledge jutted out of the structure, on which they could perch.

"Come on," Kai urged.

Reaching the ledge first, he turned and pulled her up. And then they were on top of it, standing on an uneven, natural platform. A few loose pebbles skittered over the edge, clacking off the side of the formation. Fighting dizziness, Neena looked down at how far they'd climbed.

They'd made it thirty feet from the ground.

Inching close to the formation, they clung to the steep rock's face, scanning the desert. The gaping holes below them looked like a pair of uneven eyes. Smooth sand at the top gave way to darker sand beneath. The tunnels reminded Neena of playing as a child outside of her colony, imagining the underground fortresses she might build. Those were good memories.

But this sight — and the mangled carcass — filled her with dread.

Almost everything in the desert was covered in a thin film of the sandstorm's dust, but they saw better than they could on the ground. In the west, east, and south, the desert seemed to go on forever, filled with dunes. But the northern side of the rock — behind them — was a blind spot. That made her nervous.

Finally, Kai said, "Over there. Do you see that?"

Neena followed his gaze to a few discolorations in the desert.

"More breaches," Kai said.

A pit in her stomach grew worse. "It got ahead of us in the night."

Kai nodded. "We should stay here awhile, just to be safe."

Looking down the thirty-foot face of rock, Neena asked, "Can it reach us up here?"

"I've seen it burst from the ground higher than this ledge," Kai admitted.

Neena nodded. Looking up, she saw no higher ledges on the steep spire. She wasn't sure what came next, but every instinct told her to stay off the sand.

Chapter 20: Gideon

G IDEON WALKED THE PATH AT the end of the crop rows, looking over the dusted, buried, or wilted vegetables. Even the long retaining walls, made of rock and mud, hadn't shielded the vegetables from the wind and the sand. But that was always the way, with a storm as severe as this. Between the rows, the Crop Tenders knelt, cleaning off the crops that could be cleaned, or tugging out those that were too damaged to grow any further. A stringy-haired woman tossed a handful of green vegetables into a cart. Next to her, a gaunt man dusted off a sagging, brown root. The damaged crops would be passed out as early rations.

The storm — and the deaths — would lower the morale of his people.

But Gideon couldn't let it consume them.

Grief and despair wouldn't feed stomachs.

He looked over his shoulder. A row behind him, Wyatt watched some workers load several wagons. Three rows past, Brody, Saurab, and Horatio spoke with the crop supervisors about the plans for distribution. The supervisors and Crop Tenders did their duties with a diligence that showed they knew the importance of their work.

The Crop Tenders were handpicked, expected to keep pace, or be demoted. Some of their families had done their duty for generations, passing their knowledge down to their offspring. In exchange for tending the crops, the Crop Tenders received their share of rations, as well as meat from the tithing storehouse at the front of the colony. The Crop Tenders escaped the heat and danger of the desert—it was better than being a hunter; that was for sure.

They had a special privilege.

Just like his Watchers.

Breaking from his observations, Wyatt strode past a line of carts to join Gideon.

"About ten percent of our crops are damaged," he reported, with a serious expression. Gideon could see him running figures in his head. He already had his book out, ready to make tallies.

Gideon looked from the crops across the river to the clusters of houses, where children played, and women carried buckets. Not for the first time, he wondered about the hunters caught in the desert. Depending on how they fared, he might have to speak more words at tomorrow's ceremony.

"What are we doing about the lost Crop Tenders?" Gideon asked.

"I already have supervisors working on their replacements," Wyatt told him. "The positions should be filled soon."

Gideon nodded. Wyatt performed his tasks without question, like most of Gideon's good men.

"We'll need to fix some parts of our retaining walls," Gideon observed, pointing at some fallen or scattered rocks.

"We'll get on that," Wyatt confirmed.

Gideon glanced from the crops to the top of the cliffs, watching a few men stroll the high ledges, checking the horizon. Whispers of the lost crops would permeate the colony long before the damaged rations did.

Hunger led to unrest.

It always did.

Catching Wyatt's attention, he said, "Tell Thorne to have The Watchers keep a close eye on the colony. We don't need any violence or disturbances, in the wake of empty stomachs."

Chapter 21: Raj

"**W**HERE ARE WE GOING?" ASKED Samel, struggling to keep up with Raj.

Raj toted the empty bucket in his hands, cutting from Helgid's alley and heading north, curving around several women carrying shovels and buckets. All around him, people dispersed in different directions, but most headed south, toward the riverbanks, to procure mud and straw. Raj and Samel were supposed to get materials, too, but Raj had another idea in mind first.

"I'm heading for the tithing houses," Raj said, answering Samel's question. "Maybe we'll see Neena coming back."

Samel nodded. For every one of Raj's long strides, he took several quicker steps, keeping up without complaint. Samel could be annoying, but he was a good companion. Raj wove around a few elderly people, hobbling from their dwellings. A few glanced at Raj and Samel with the scrutinizing stares that old people always gave kids their age.

Getting to the center of the colony, they rounded the enormous, circular Comm Building. The round, curved roof rose higher than any of the hovels around it. The sturdy walls seemed impenetrable. Even the long, straight annex that jutted out from the side seemed as if it could withstand the worst sandstorm. Raj could never imagine it falling.

He saw none of The Heads of Colony.

Good, he thought with relief.

Gideon and his important men always made him nervous.

The path split in two, curving around the Comm Building and reforming. Raj chose a path east, with less people, and curved back around to the main path. In the distance, past the clusters of people, he saw the edges of the tithing houses. To their left and right, out of sight, were the storehouses. Beyond them, the path lost its shape and melded with the sand.

Two towering spires sat on either side of that path, about half a klick after the colony ended. Raj had always thought of those structures as two sides of a large door, welcoming the returning hunters. Farther out in the desert, more spires rose in intermittent places, like enormous spears thrust into the ground. Most were far enough away that he could only see their silhouettes under the sun.

Often, he saw hunters coming up that path, dragging game, or hauling larger bags than what they'd gone out with. More than once, Raj welcomed Neena as she came up that path, always with a smile and a tearful embrace.

Hoping for a similar reunion, he walked faster, temporarily forgetting his brother's smaller legs.

Movement from an adjacent alley caught Raj's attention.

He looked right.

A tight cluster of kids wormed their way past some adults, pointing and yelling.

Pointing at Raj and Samel.

"Hey!" they shouted.

Bailey and his friends.

A group of children became a mob, shoes slapping the alley as they ran. Their shouts grew bolder. A few adults looked at the children with mild annoyance. To them, the running mob was nothing more than kids engaged in play.

Raj knew better.

Fear spiked in his stomach as he grabbed Samel's hand, pulling him in the other direction. "Come on!"

"Where are we going, Raj?"

Raj didn't answer.

His heart slammed against his ribcage as he chose the path of least resistance, cutting away and north. He clutched his bucket with his other hand. They ran through a smaller alley, startling some people who moved out of the way, or bumping a few who didn't react in time. Some people wheeled pushcarts, while others carried children. Cries of anger and annoyance followed their path.

Raj had no time for apologies.

A few men held up a carcass near their house, preparing to skin it. The fleeting thought came to Raj that he would've asked them if they had seen his sister, if a bloodthirsty group of kids weren't chasing them.

He lost hold of Samel.

Too late, he looked back.

Samel crashed against a pushcart, knocking over the man behind it. The cart overturned. Stones hit the ground and rolled. More people stepped back, caught in the middle of an unexpected scene.

"You filthy rats!" the man yelled, staggering to his feet.

"We're sorry!" Raj said, helping his brother up.

"You'll be sorry when you help me pick up all these stones!"

Raj glanced over his shoulder, catching sight of Bailey and his friends in the distance. The commotion had given them away.

"Come on!" Raj said, clutching Samel's hand and his bucket as they ran, ignoring the man's angry cries behind them.

They wound through another few alleys, catching sight of the kids running behind them, or hearing their fast footsteps. More and more people glanced in their direction.

The bystanders' attention was drawing the kids. Bailey and his gang only had to follow the stares. Frantic, Raj pushed on, until quiet surrounded them.

With panic, Raj realized they had ended up in the Crop Tenders section. Most were at work down by the river.

No one was here.

He paused for a split second, looking at a few closed doors on the houses on either side of the alley, wishing they could get inside. But those doors would be locked.

Samel clutched his winded stomach, frightened tears glistening in his eyes.

"I can't run anymore, Raj!" Samel said, shaking.

"We have to move!" Raj urged. Looking sideways, he had an idea. "Behind one of these houses. We'll hide before they see us!"

"Caught you, orphan boy!"

Raj's blood froze.

He turned.

Bailey and five other boys stood farther down the alley. All had hungry expressions of violence on their faces. More voices shouted in the distance as the rest of the pack rounded an intersecting alley, reaching threateningly for their knives, or clenching their fists. The boys took a few steps as they saw an end to their chase.

Hiding was out.

Raj's heart slammed into his ribs as he surveyed more boys than he could handle, knife at his side or not.

"Let's settle this, orphan boy!" Bailey shouted. Triumph bled through his words. "Stop running, and I'll spare your pissy-pants brother!"

"Come on, girly boy!"

A few of Bailey's friends yelled similar taunts.

If it were a fair fight, Raj might've considered taking on the older boy, pulling his knife in a threat he couldn't finish. But these boys didn't play fair.

Frantic, Raj turned and assessed the area. No one could help. All they could do was turn and flee.

"Come on, Sam!"

Their footsteps reverberated off the empty alley as they continued fleeing, past lifeless hovels with closed doors, more empty alleys, and pushcarts filled with sand. They kept their focus straight ahead. A lost step would put them closer to a fist, or maybe even a knife. Samel struggled to match Raj's quicker pace, gasping for air.

Catching sight of an alley, Raj veered for it.

He slammed into a thick, meaty chest.

He fell back on his butt, stunned, into the main alley.

Raj looked from the ground to the face of a stern, muscular man he'd seen several times at the base of the cliffs or walking alongside Gideon and The Heads of Colony. *A Watcher.* The man frowned, his gaze wandering from Raj to Samel, as Samel frantically tugged at Raj's arm, trying to pull him up.

"Come on, Raj!"

"What's going on?" the man demanded, loudly enough that Samel stopped pulling.

"Nothing." Raj could hardly formulate an answer.

The man looked past him into the main alley, where Bailey and his friends stopped stiff in the center of the path. A few of them relaxed their hands to their sides. One by one, their malicious faces turned into a fearful respect.

"Are you Crop Tenders' children?" the Watcher called.

Raj turned over his shoulder, watching a few of the boys' slack-jawed expressions. Finding courage, one or two shook their heads.

"Get out of here, then!" The Watcher raised a threatening arm.

The boys delayed a moment, as if the man's words might be a test, and then feet were moving and heads were looking over shoulders. The Watcher stared after the fleeing boys for a long moment, before turning his attention to Raj and Samel.

"Why are you here?" he demanded.

Feeling the weight of the man's eyes, Raj said, "We're getting materials to fix our house." He looked down at his bucket.

"Shouldn't you be at the river?" the man asked.

"Yes, sir," Raj said.

He stared at Raj with a stern expression. For a moment, Raj was certain he would rip them away to The Heads of Colony. Finally, he said, "Get to it, then."

Raj scrambled to his feet and took a step backward. He watched the man, as if The Watcher might change his mind, but the man turned and stormed away without a word.

Chapter 22: Raj

RAJ AND SAMEL HURRIED THROUGH the streets until they reached an area filled with people. Raj's heart still beat loudly from the chase, and their encounter with The Watcher. Thankfully, he saw no sign of Bailey and his friends. He and Samel continued until they were far beyond the place where they'd been chased.

When they had made enough distance that Raj's legs no longer shook, Samel asked, "Is that Watcher going to tell Gideon about us?"

"I don't think so," Raj said, hoping that were true.

Samel still looked afraid.

Both of them knew the stories about those who had been caught fighting, stealing, or disrupting others' work. Gideon and his men were strict. Causing a commotion was an easy way to land in a cell, or worse. Raj recalled the rumors of a man who had stabbed and killed another over a sprig of taproot, many years ago. If the stories were to be believed, that man had been cast out and never seen again.

Even the simple-minded boys like Bailey knew better than to run up on one of Gideon's trusted men.

"Are you sure they won't cast us out?" Samel asked.

Raj swallowed. "I don't think so."

He looked over their shoulders, as if he might find The Watcher following them, but the alley was empty. Even if they told The Watcher the truth, Bailey had enough boys around him to corroborate a lie. He and Samel were better off keeping their mouths shut.

Swallowing, Raj worked his way west through the colony, getting far enough to see the river in the distance. Still no Bailey.

"Aren't we going home?" Samel asked.

"We need materials for Helgid," Raj said.

"Materials?" Samel spoke as if Raj talked of a venomous beast.

Seeing the frightened look on Samel's face, he said, "I don't think Bailey and the others will bother us — at least not now. You saw how The Watcher scared them. We should be safe."

"We should tell Helgid what happened," Samel said, waiting for agreement.

Raj sighed and shook his head. "What can she do?"

"Maybe she can stop them."

"Helgid is as likely to be thrown in a cell as us," Raj said. "We can't drag her into this."

"Maybe she can tell those boys to stop. Maybe they'll listen to her."

"She might say some words, but you heard how they spoke about her. They don't care what she has to say." Softening his tone, Raj said, "We shouldn't involve her, Samel. We'll handle our own problems, like we always have. Like Neena taught us. We'll be fine."

"You promise, Raj?" Samel asked, looking up at his brother with innocent eyes.

"I promise."

Chapter 23: Neena

NEENA LOOKED DOWN THE ROCKY spire at the fawn's mutilated remains. Fear coursed through her, as she said, "The blood looks fresh. My guess is that the Abomination killed the fawn this morning."

Kai nodded gravely.

"I think it was related to the Rydeer," she added.

"What do you mean?" Kai asked.

Neena quietly told the story of the game she'd almost caught, until the sandstorm surprised her. She told how she had spared the fawn's life, fearing it would die without its mother. Of course, that didn't matter now.

Even from their high perch, Neena saw the thick cloud of flies swarming and descending, laying their eggs. More scavenging animals besides birds wouldn't be far behind. In a land so desolate, no creature refused an easy meal.

Looking at the ground, she pictured the enormous Abomination bursting up, bashing through the ledge on which they stood, and knocking them into its mouth.

Kai's words about his hunting party came back to her.

I heard the screams. I saw the creature swallow them whole, as it erupted from the ground.

Neena stared south, in the direction of her colony. Red Rock was still two full days' travel away. Thinking of her colony reminded her of the hunters she'd seen on a hilltop two days ago. Those men were probably close to home by now. After a sandstorm as bad as this one, they would've cut their trips short to check on their families.

Or maybe they were food for the monster.

A shiver of dread ran through her. The next mangled body they found might be one of her colonists. The other hunters might not respect her, but she didn't wish a death like that on anyone.

They drank their water sparingly, waiting in silence for a long while, shifting positions occasionally, when their legs grew tired. The perch was wide enough to fit them adequately, but not comfortably. More than once, Neena caught her balance so she wouldn't fall.

The desert held an eerie silence.

It felt as if the landscape was holding its breath.

Neena saw no sign of rats, or even the squawking birds that had left earlier.

She couldn't imagine how Kai had spent days like this, living in a constant state of dread. The toll was evident in the circles beneath his eyes, and in his dirty, ripped clothes. She could hear it in his voice, after the days and nights he'd spent in the desert.

Something rumbled.

Neena gripped the wall tightly.

She looked at Kai.

Fear awakened in his eyes as he scanned from east to west.

The rumble came again—faint, but loudly enough that they knew they had heard it. Neena clutched her knife in a sweaty hand. Her heart beat like a trip hammer as she searched the legions of brown dunes. The sun's obscuring rays turned the desert into a mirage; any of those sand hills could actually be a monster, coming to eat them.

Below them, the stream trickled faintly.

The dark holes were entrances to some dark, horrific world.

They waited several tense moments, not moving, not breathing.

Slowly, Kai raised his hand to point toward the desert. *He'd found something.* Neena followed his finger to the source of his attention: a small, moving dot in the distance going east to west. It was some sort of animal, though it was impossible to tell the species. The animal was small and far enough away that it appeared to be going slowly, but she could tell it was going fast. Another Rydeer, perhaps, or a wolf.

The dot picked up speed, heading behind one of the distant dunes.

She lost sight of it.

Neena adjusted on the ledge, trying to see past the giant mount of sand. Slowly, she and Kai shuffled.

A boom echoed across the desert.

A spray of sand shot up from behind the dune.

A long, piercing screech echoed across the landscape, cutting short in a squeal of agony. Neena's hand flew to her mouth, trapping in a cry she'd never let out.

The sand rained back to the ground, settling behind the dune.

Kai mouthed words she didn't need him to speak. *Stay put, stay put...*

Chapter 24: Raj

LUSTERS OF PEOPLE WAITED IN line, talking, or corralling their young ones. A few of the older children splashed near the riverbanks while their parents waited with their buckets. Men talked loudly about the work they'd done on their homes, or the work left to be finished.

Raj and Samel took a spot at the end of the line.

Setting down his bucket, Raj watched some people heading for a favored spot on the riverbank to scoop mud.

Samel shifted from foot to foot. Every so often, he looked up the path.

Filling the silence with nervous conversation, Samel asked, "Do you think we'll be back at Helgid's for supper?"

"I hope," Raj said, as he followed Samel's gaze.

Squinting to see through the late-afternoon glare, Raj saw three silhouettes coming down to the river. He tensed, until he realized they were hunters. Two of them walked close together, talking and hefting full bags. Another man hung back behind them. All were dressed in brown and white pants and shirts and carried long, sharp spears.

"Hunters," Raj said, calling Samel's attention to them.

"Do you think they've seen Neena?" Samel asked, temporarily forgetting some of his anxiety.

"It's possible," Raj said. Making the quick determination that they weren't getting any closer in line, and that Bailey and his friends weren't around, he added, "Why don't we go ask them?"

Abandoning their position at the end of the line, they approached the hunters.

The two men in front unwrapped their shawls, revealing their sweaty, bearded faces. They laughed at a joke Raj and Samel had missed. The last person walked more slowly, having trouble carrying his burden.

Approaching the last one, Raj said, "Hello, sir."

The man removed his shawl, revealing a patchy beard and a cocky smile. He made a show of adjusting his bag. "Come to see how it's done, eh?"

Hoping to bolster the man's ego, Raj said, "It sounds as if the hunt was successful."

"I caught a big, fat Rydeer." The man grinned. "I speared it myself."

"Where was it?"

The man cranked a thumb over his shoulder. "About a day's travel north. It was drinking near a spring."

"It sounds as if you are skilled," Raj complimented.

"I am." The man smiled, revealing a mouthful of crooked teeth. "I can throw a spear faster than an animal can run. Perhaps I can give you some tips, when you get older."

"I'd like that." Sensing his opportunity, Raj asked, "Do you mind if I ask you about something?"

"Sure, what is it?"

"I was wondering if you'd seen my sister," Raj said, trying to disguise his worry.

Before the man could answer, the others turned and approached.

"Who's he looking for?" one of them overheard, wiping some greasy sweat from his brow.

"His sister," the younger man repeated.

The two older men exchanged curt smiles. Seeing them

up close, Raj recognized them from previous run-ins. It seemed as if they recognized him, too.

"Your sister?" One of the older men laughed. "Shouldn't she be down by the river?"

The first man chuckled.

"She was out hunting, like you," Raj said, sticking his chin out the way he'd seen grown men do. "I was hoping she was heading back after the storm."

"If she was in the storm, she'd better have held onto her spear," the bearded man said, making a show of grabbing his crotch. The others laughed.

Perhaps trying to curry favor with the older men, the first hunter said, "Maybe the wind carried her up to the twin moons."

More laughter.

"Wait a moment," one of the men piped up, before Raj and Samel could leave. "I think I saw her."

A small hope filled Raj's stomach. "You did?"

"She was the one with the baby under her shawl, wasn't she?" he asked, unable to hide his coy smile, as he held one of his arms to his breast and rocked it back and forth.

"Never mind," Raj said, pulling Samel's arm. "We'll find her ourselves."

Together, he and Samel walked back to the line, resuming their wait for the straw.

Chapter 25: Raj

ELGID STOOD FROM THE HEARTH as she saw Raj and Samel coming through the door, setting down some utensils and brushing off her hands. She smiled.

"Long line at the river?" she asked knowingly.

"Yes." Raj hefted his heavy bucket to show her the water and mud inside. He traded a knowing look with Samel, who carried the straw.

"How many were waiting?"

"A few hundred."

"After a storm like this, it is no wonder. Thank you for sparing an old woman's back." Helgid made a show of grimacing.

Raj smiled. Her kind words were meant to make him and Samel feel useful. Still, he appreciated the compliment.

"I'll make some broth for dinner," she said.

Glancing at the wall, where Helgid had stuffed the broken pieces earlier, Raj asked, "We should have enough material to fix all the holes."

"That sounds great," Helgid said, filling one of her pots with water. "We can start on them after supper."

Turning with his bucket, Raj ran his fingers over one of the holes, gauging the size.

He recalled a storm a few months ago, when he and Neena had worked together, repairing several holes in the walls in their own house, while Samel laughed and played.

That memory gave him a wave of nostalgia that deepened his worry. He prayed she'd be home soon.

"I almost forgot something," Helgid said, picking up a spoon.

"What is it?" Raj asked, turning.

"You had a visitor."

"Me?" At first, Raj thought she was speaking of Neena. Then he recalled The Watcher's stern expression, and his strong, waving hand. What if the intimidating man had thought better of his warning, and come to rip them away?

"It was a girl."

"A...girl?" Raj's brow furrowed in surprise.

"The one you helped this morning," Helgid said. "She came to say thank you."

Raj recalled the frantic girl who had been outside the home, and her mournful tears. He didn't even know her name. In the frenzy of the moment, there hadn't been time to catch it. He looked from Helgid to the door, as if the girl might be standing there, unnoticed. Of course, she wasn't.

"She left a while ago," Helgid clarified. "But she wanted me to give you this."

Helgid reached into the folds of her shawl, pulling out a round, shiny piece of metal. Raj walked over tentatively, receiving a gift he hadn't expected.

"What is it?"

"She said it was one of her grandmother's keepsakes," Helgid explained. "She saved it from the rubble, along with a few other personal items, before The Watchers carried away the remnants of her grandmother's building. She wanted you to have it."

Raj opened his hand and took it. The piece of metal had several strange markings on its surface. A few indents on its sides contained some crusted sand. The object looked as if it was in its original state — unmelted, perhaps even whole. *Maybe it has looked the same for generations*, Raj thought with awe. Rarely did the colonists own anything that they couldn't find an obvious use for. As his father used to say, waste was a luxury for the heavens.

He swallowed as he turned the unique piece in his hand.

"Can I see it?" Samel asked. Curiosity got the better of him as he peered over Raj's outstretched hand.

"Did the girl say what it was?" Raj asked Helgid.

"No," Helgid said. "She only knew that her grandmother had kept it for many years. It meant something to her. She thought that you should have it, for assisting her."

Raj nodded, trying to envision the dead woman as she had looked alive, rather than a sand-covered, lifeless body. Perhaps she was in the heavens and watching them right now. That thought gave him warmth he hadn't felt in a long while. It was certainly better than the fear that had accompanied him for most of the afternoon.

"Did you catch the girl's name?" Raj asked.

"It was a nice name," Helgid said. "I think it was Adriana."

"Adriana," Raj repeated, feeling more of the same warmth. "Do you know where she lives?"

Helgid looked as if she was trying to remember. "Next to the house where you pulled out her grandmother, I think."

Raj closed his fist around the object, then opened his fingers again, unable to stop staring at the wondrous piece. "I should thank her," he said.

"She was off to visit some of the other people who helped, so you might not find her now," Helgid said. "Perhaps tomorrow morning would be the best time to catch her, after the ceremony."

Raj reluctantly agreed, even though he wanted nothing more than to leave and thank the girl now.

He couldn't erase a thought from his mind, as he looked at the piece in his hand. Had the other people who assisted her received strange gifts, too?

Chapter 26: Gideon

IDEON STOOD IN THE CENTER of the Comm Building's main room. For once, he was away from the bustle of his people, away from The Heads of Colony. Most were outside, finishing the last of their duties. He looked up at the ceiling. A few nicks and marks on the building's exterior told the story of yesterday's storm, but thankfully, they had no large holes to patch.

More importantly, none of his men were injured.

Cherishing a rare, quiet moment, Gideon slicked back his gray hair, clearing the sweat of a busy day from his brow. His bones ached from a long day of standing and thinking. Too many decisions weighed on his mind. Sitting at a chair by the round table, he thought them over.

As his father had taught him, an overlooked detail was better caught early.

He kept an absent eye on the strange, round piece of the satellite dish as he rolled the plans of the day over in his head. Most of the damaged crops had been ferreted out and sorted. The Crop Tenders had brought them to the secured storehouse at the front of the colony, where The Watchers could keep an eye on them. Tomorrow, the Crop Tenders would distribute them to the hungry colonists.

All that was left was to speak his words at the ceremony.

Gideon thought about the speech he'd recited too many times. Those consoling euphemisms, written by his forefathers and spoken at every ceremony, would help the

colonists grieve. Gideon didn't believe half of those words—
he was too jaded to believe something existed, other than a
sky full of stars and a ground that was too easy to be buried
in—but the words were necessary.

Having a predictable pattern made some of the simple-
minded colonists forget the fact that they were stuck on a
world in which things never got better.

Routine deflected chaos.

Once the colonists awoke in the morning and ate their
breakfasts, he would lead his people to the graveyard, along
with the other Heads of Colony, alleviating the grief from
the storm.

Afterward, they would move on.

He hoped.

Chapter 27: Neena

THE SUN CAST A REDDISH-ORANGE glow, creating a majestic back light over the horizon as daylight faded. If Neena's throat weren't so parched, she would've appreciated the beauty of sunset, as she did on some of those rare, fruitful days after hunting.

For the rest of the afternoon, she and Kai had sweated under the sun, tipping the last of the flasks they'd refilled before climbing, watching the light fade. They'd seen no sign of the creature and heard no rumbles. Over time, a few scavenging birds had returned to the carcass, continuing their meal.

The story of whatever they'd seen behind the dunes was hidden, for now.

At the moment, they had a more pressing concern: they needed more water.

Enacting the plan that they'd whispered about for most of the afternoon, Neena looked over the ledge at the dead fawn.

"I'll go first," she whispered, to a nod from Kai.

Without another word, she turned and put her foot on a firm rock, slowly lowering herself. Neena steadied her shaking hands as she descended, feeling the burn in her calves as she tried keeping her balance. As soon as she was a body's width away, Kai followed her down the sheer face. Neena kept her eyes on the rocks as she gripped tightly.

She felt weaker than when she'd made the climb. She

was dehydrated. But an entire night without water would weaken them further.

They had no choice but to take a risk.

The thought of whatever had died behind the dune came back to her, as she relived the shrieking, agonizing cries of pain. She held her breath, avoiding a betraying noise and trying to forget about whatever lurked in the desert.

She was halfway down the formation when a piece of stone cracked underneath her boot. Neena stopped, clung to the rock face, and listened to the stone ping to the bottom, landing in the stream with a plunk.

Above her, Kai halted. The air held the same, eerie calm that occurred this afternoon.

Somewhere out of sight, one of the feeding birds flapped its wings. It squawked, but didn't fly away.

Exhaling, Neena continued. She kept an eye on the ground, not ready to trust anything in the semi-darkness. Finally, she eased herself onto the jutting crag, climbed back and over it, and landed softly. Kai followed.

Neena walked heel to toe in the sand, attentive for squeaks in her boots. Kai followed. Reaching the stream, they knelt, filled their flasks, and gently drank. After a long day in the heat, the water felt like a heavenly miracle. Neena sipped until she was full, but she didn't gorge. After topping their flasks again, they quietly stood.

Getting close to her, Kai whispered, "Are you ready?"

Neena nodded.

She looked over at the dark crevices in the ground, which seemed even darker with daylight dying.

Neena took one of her small game bags from her pack and walked purposefully toward the dead fawn, keeping an eye on the gaping holes. Too many shadows surrounded them. Seeing her coming, the birds cawed and scattered. Neena swallowed as she reached the fawn, knelt, and waved away some of the stubborn flies.

She only needed a few moments.

Holding her breath from the growing stench of the meat, she bent down, using her knife to carve away some of the untouched parts of the carcass's fur, finding the fresher meat beneath. When she had cut through the fawn's top layers, she sliced out a few pieces, stuffed them in her game bag, and walked away.

With full flasks and meat in her bag, she and Kai returned up the rock face.

Neena and Kai huddled on the ledge, chewing pieces of the raw, soft fawn. The same reservations that had kept Kai from building a fire stopped them now. Even if they had wood to burn, they wouldn't use it.

"The meat isn't so bad, once you get used to it," Kai said, with a grim smile.

She smiled back, trying to control her nausea.

The meat wasn't tasty, but it was palatable, when faced with the option of starving. She remembered what Kai had told her about getting sick. She worried about that. But it was too late now.

Underneath her worry was a small sense of accomplishment. At least they had made it back up to relative safety, away from the ground and the ominous holes.

They sat in silence, filling their stomachs.

The light of the twin moons cast a nascent glow over the landscape. Somewhere beneath them, the birds returned to the carcass. Every so often, she heard them pecking and shifting. Those sounds were unnerving, but the proximity of the birds meant the creature wasn't near.

She hoped.

Swallowing a mouthful of bland meat, Neena washed it

down with water. Neither she nor Kai had suggested leaving during the night.

They knew it was too dangerous.

Kai's face was little more than a silhouette under the twin moons as he finished his food. "We will have another decision to make in the morning, assuming we live that long."

"A decision?"

"We will need to figure out where we're headed." He looked out over the desert.

Another unspoken conversation bubbled to the surface.

In the time they'd traveled, survival had taken priority over any other decisions. But now Neena's buried worries came rushing back. She was traveling with a man she barely knew — a man from a strange colony — taking him in the direction of her home. Was she really going to bring him to Red Rock? How would they react?

"You seem as if you are thinking about something," Kai said.

"I'm worried about my brothers. Ever since I saw that creature, I have the desperate urge to get back to them, to make sure they're all right." Neena looked at him.

"And that makes you wonder whether you should bring me," he said, taking an intuitive leap.

Neena sighed. "Until yesterday, I knew nothing about New Canaan, or this beast. And then I met you, and everything changed. Now I have worries I did not have before." She looked at Kai. "It seems only death lurks in the desert."

Kai fell silent a moment. "It would make the most sense to head to Red Rock, but I don't want to put you in an awkward position."

Neena sighed. Voicing her uncertainties gave her a strange sense of guilt. "If I arrive with a stranger, I am uncertain how my people will react. I am uncertain if they will even believe the story we have to tell. And I have a deeper concern." A pang of dread kept Neena from speaking.

"What?" Kai asked.

She exhaled a nervous breath. "What if we think the creature is gone, only to have it appear at my colony? What if we bring death back with us?"

Kai fell silent, obviously concerned about the same thing. "I do not have a good answer for that."

Neena wrung her hands. She imagined Kai's ten dead companions in the desert, crushed or eaten. What if she decided to bring Kai back, and they both brought the Abomination to Red Rock?

"Perhaps we can split up. That way, one of us is safe," Kai suggested. "The creature has followed me longer. Perhaps it will recognize something in my vibrations, and I can lead it away. Perhaps it never has to reach your people at all."

Realizing the implication behind his words, Neena said, "Are you saying we part ways, and you will search for New Canaan?"

"I brought the creature here. Maybe I can lead it away. Maybe later, I will find New Canaan again."

Neena backpedaled his suggestion. "I don't know if wandering around in the desert is the answer."

"Perhaps I can travel so far away that it will never return at all." Kai's voice cracked, as he looked away, out into the darkening desert, obviously thinking of his dead companions. "Maybe that is what I should have done days ago. Just say the word, and I will leave and not follow you. I swear by the twin moons."

Neena looked out over the desert—a desert that concealed the beast. She felt an empathetic worry for Kai that she couldn't explain.

"Your leaving is no guarantee that I will escape," she

said. "It might kill you and come for me afterward. Or it might follow me, instead."

Kai opened and closed his mouth, but he didn't refute her concern.

"Or maybe it will find someone else from my colony." Neena shuddered as another buried fear rose to the surface. "What if it stumbles on another hunter, like me? Someone else might bring it back before we do."

"It was a thought I was afraid to voice," Kai admitted.

A new thought struck her. "What if I die before I warn my people? What will happen to my brothers?"

Considering her own death gave Neena a strange feeling.

If she never made it back, what would happen to Raj and Samel?

Most hunters had families who would look for them, but Neena's family had no one.

They had Helgid, sure, but she was an old woman, in no condition to trek into the desert. And if no one helped, that meant Raj and Samel were alone. Neena pictured Raj and Samel in the desert, wandering aimlessly and coming across the beast instead, meeting the same fate as the Rydeer and its fawn. She felt a wave of fear greater than the worry for her own safety.

Raj and Samel might die, and then others might die, too.

"Anyone who searches for me might bring it back with them," she concluded, following her thought to a decision. "I need to get back to my people. I need to warn them. And right now, you know more about this creature than anyone. I think it only makes sense that you come back with me."

"Are you certain?"

"It is the only answer that seems right," Neena said resolutely.

"I do not know of a way to kill it," Kai reminded her. "I am not sure how much help I can be."

"No, but if my people are aware of it, maybe they can

take precautions," Neena said. "Perhaps our warning can save more people from death."

"Thank you again for your help," Kai said.

"Do not thank me until we make it back alive," Neena said, returning his grim smile.

Kai nodded in the darkness. Sitting next to him, Neena felt a small wave of comfort in a large, empty desert. With their decision made, Kai shifted, probably thinking through the implications of their decision. "What will your people say, when they see me?"

"They will have no choice but to listen," Neena said, praying that was true. "They have to."

Chapter 28: Darius

D ARIUS HOBBLED AROUND HIS HOME under torchlight, clutching his pack and listening to the last of the loud voices outside. One or two colonists lingered near their homes, finalizing the last of their patchwork. Soon, they would be indoors for the evening, huddling by their hearths and cooking dinner. Later, they would settle into an exhaustive sleep after a trying day, squeezing their children and thanking the heavens for their good luck.

Darius had other plans.

Creeping over to one of the bins he had secured earlier, he opened it and tucked some items in his bag. He pulled out a few spears and knives and placed them back on his bench, where their owners could find them, should the worst happen.

When he finished packing, he tested the weight of the bag on his old shoulders. The goods never seemed to get any lighter. But then, they never did. Despite his aging body, Darius's mind felt the same as when he was a young man.

It was a cruel trick from the heavens about which he and Elmer often joked.

Opening another bin, Darius pulled out a long, sharpened knife he reserved for occasions such as this, slipped it into his sheath, and removed several torches, sticking them into his bag. He closed the sack in such a way that they hung out in easy reach.

Walking to the wall, he stared at the old, nostalgic spear.

The long weapon would be no good in close quarters. His knife would be better.

Darius ambled over to his workbench, stuffed some dried vegetables into his mouth, and waited for the bustle of evening activity to give way to the flutter of bats.

Then he crept to the door and slipped out among them.

Under the cover of darkness, Darius snuck through Red Rock, quietly moving with his cane. The houses around him were little more than silhouettes under the light of the twin moons. Most of the haze had gone, but a thin layer hung in the air, giving him extra cover. Darius stuck to the shadows, using a lifetime of familiarity to guide him toward the eastern rock formation. Every so often, the skittering of a night creature made him pause, but none were loud enough to signify a notable threat.

He peered through the dark, finding a few bits of ambient light. A few times, he saw a glow under the cracks of hovels' doorways, but none of the lights moved, and none of the doors opened. Most in the colony were asleep, except The Watchers.

Darius stared up toward the moonlit cliffs, locating a few stationary torches. Only the bravest Watchers worked so late a shift. With their visibility limited, only a few observant ears were needed to listen for sandstorms.

Everyone knew the cliffs were even more dangerous at night than during the day.

For most of the night shifts, The Watchers trolled the alleys, searching for predators that wandered into Red Rock. Their shifts were dull, but occasionally, they encountered a speckled wolf prowling the shadows, or a dust beetle that was big enough to wake some of the colonists. Of the scarce animals that lived nearby, most were savvy enough to stay away from the colony.

All had learned to fear humans, except those in the caves.

Darius swallowed as a memory came back to him — as fresh and haunting as it had been two years prior.

He'd never forget the day he'd learned that Akron was missing. He'd been in his house, fixing spears, when he heard commotion. Breaking from his work, he went outside to discover his neighbors conversing with The Watchers. Akron's parents had reported him missing, and a search had begun.

Some in Darius's position might've kept hold of the damning information they had, but not him. As soon as he heard about the boy's disappearance, Darius had admitted his knowledge of Akron's exploration of the tunnels, thinking he might help.

The leaders had refused his assistance.

The Heads of Colony — and The Watchers — had forbidden him from going into the caves and helping with the search. No sooner had he spoken than people blamed him for the boy's interest in those prohibited explorations — especially the boy's parents, who had never let him forget, either in the days after, or the days since.

The Watchers had searched the caves for a while, but they never found Akron.

Eventually, everyone had accepted that the boy was dead, including the boy's parents, who hated Darius and wished him dead, too. Most days, Darius hated himself. His guilt ate away at him. If he had somehow slipped past The Watchers on those first days, perhaps he could've found the boy in time to save him. Of course, there was no chance that Akron was alive now.

All he could hope for was a proper burial.

Moving through the dark alleys, Darius kept an eye out

for any of The Watchers' torches moving in his direction. Years of traveling in darkened conditions had ingrained a sense in him that he couldn't explain. Sometimes, it felt as if Darius had an animal's instincts. On nights like these, he was grateful for them.

Soon, he reached the last of the houses in a row.

Pausing to adjust his bag, he looked up at the cliffs. None of the torch lights had moved position. The alleys around him were as dark as the ones behind.

Seeing nothing suspicious, he trekked through the sand to the eastern rock formation and into the closest cave entrance. When he was far enough inside to avoid notice, he reached for a torch, lit it, and made his way deeper, undetected.

Chapter 29: Darius

DARIUS GLANCED BEHIND HIM, ENSURING no one followed. The flame of his torch lit the smooth, auburn walls of the tunnel on either side. Sticks and rocks covered the cave floor. Often, the children of Red Rock threw items into the cave when they thought no one was looking. Some acted on dares, proving their courage to the others, while others tested their own bravery.

Some cured their boredom with those dares.

None, except Darius, entered.

And Akron, on too many occasions, including the time he disappeared, he reminded himself.

That thought urged him on as he clutched his cane, careful not to make too much noise. Darius moved steadily, following a path he'd traveled more times than he could count. From somewhere outside and behind, he heard the hoot of a desert owl, perched on the giant formation's outer ledges. Soon, the sound disappeared, and an eerie, closed-in silence surrounded him. Darkness enveloped everything outside his torchlight.

Deep in the tunnels, there were no days and nights.

There was only the amount of water and food in one's bag, the number of torches he had, and the bravery in his heart.

Darius swallowed as he recalled the times he had traveled here as a younger man, always careful to come back before the morning, so he wouldn't be discovered. Back then, the threat of lost rations hung over his head.

Now, his punishment would be even worse.

The Heads of Colony had already warned him twice: after his shattered leg, and after Akron's death. He couldn't fathom what they would do to him now.

The rules of Gideon and his men were getting stricter. Underneath the stern demeanor of The Heads of Colony, Darius saw an undercurrent of nervousness. Each storm chipped away at their outward assurance.

Gone were the days of freedom, when young colonists might enjoy more than a handful of years without worry. He wasn't sure if it was nostalgia, or a bitter truth. Sometimes, it felt as if the planet were a river, slowly running dry, with no way to replenish itself.

Following the curved, red tunnel, Darius kept his torch high and his knife clutched in his cane hand. He knew that the sandstorms drove creatures into hiding, giving him more things to worry about than Watchers. He reached an intersection, veering left. Lifting his torch, he spotted a faded, familiar marking as high as a hand could reach. A circle.

Seeing that familiar marking triggered memories. All at once, Darius was a young man, with a limber body and a spear in his hand. In a cave that often felt menacing, the circular marking was a thick blanket, comforting him on a cold night. He smiled as he passed the familiar drawing, heading over some crushed rubble and skirting a divot large enough to grab a boot and hold onto it.

His love for the caves was tempered by his fear of their power.

A few times while sleeping in his hovel, he had awoken from some terrifying dream, where he was trapped in the suffocating darkness forever, dragging his body through a tunnel with no end. Listening to the crackle of his torch, he clutched it tighter, remembering that time when he had been without it. Darius had been lucky to make it out after his accident.

And yet he kept returning.

He followed the cave through several more turns, using his old, faded markings when he could find them, substituting memory when he couldn't. In a few places, he saw slashes on the walls from the miners. He entered a narrow section of the tunnel, bending down and leaning more heavily on his cane. More memories came back to him. He recalled Akron's stories of avoiding animals in the caves. Akron had been lucky in his travels, until he wasn't.

A pair of glowing eyes startled him.

Darius thrust his torch in front of him and froze.

A small, desert fox craned its neck and looked back at him, fear in its face. Darius held it in an uneasy glare for a moment before it raced away, burrowing into a distant hole. Rocks scattered and fell, pinging off the floor as its claws scratched something out of sight.

Darius took a few steps, finding the fox's rear end on the side of the cave. Its tail waved back and forth, and then it disappeared. He heard the echoes of its escape somewhere in the wall. It sounded as if the fox had gotten much farther than just into a small hole. Where was it?

He knew foxes found dens that were smaller than humans could navigate, but this lair sounded deep.

Heart hammering, Darius crept closer, illuminating the pile of stones the fox had kicked up.

The fox had revealed a head-sized, circular opening.

Stooping, Darius poked at the surrounding stones, loosening a few more and knocking them to the ground. A den.

Not a den, a *passage*.

He stuck his torch into the hole, illuminating a space

that went much deeper and wider than a normal animal's lair. Looking up, he saw something else.

Akron's triangular mark.

Darius bent down, making his way through the hole he'd exposed after moving more rocks. His pack scraped the ceiling. He held his knife in front of him, as if the fox might appear and nip him, but it wasn't close. Far in the distance, he heard louder echoes as it went farther away.

Darius kept crawling, fitting his old frame through the passage, leading with his cane and his knife. The cave was hot before, but now it was sweltering. The ceiling of the passage weighed down on him, pressing his bag tighter on his back. A new, panicked thought struck him.

What if he got stuck and died? He would surely die slowly.

No one except Elmer knew where he was going, and even if someone else did, who would look for him? Darius might be a fossil for someone else to discover. *Or maybe no one would ever find him.* He swallowed as he dragged his lame leg behind him. His torch illuminated an end to the narrow, uncomfortable space. Pulling himself through, he pushed with his hands and his cane, until he regained his footing and stood.

Darius was deep in a dark cave, with sides as wide as the one in which he'd traveled.

He looked left and right, down two sides of a tunnel he'd never explored.

Darius felt as if he was on to something more promising than he'd ever found. But which way should he go? The last thing he wanted was an encounter with a cornered, scared fox.

After some debate, he chose a path to the right, combing through the tunnel, stopping every so often to check for revealing marks. He saw no more triangles. He kept going, ignoring the pain in his joints and leg, stooping or shimmying as needed. The tunnel walls were a blend of auburn, with mixes of brown, or occasionally black, where varieties of rock blended together.

Eventually, the tunnel rose, seemingly headed toward the surface. Darius followed it until he found a sliver of light.

A breeze told him he had reached an exit.

He slowed, wondering where he had ended up. Ducking beneath a low-hanging crag, he peered into a seemingly empty desert, illuminated by the light of the moons.

He saw no sign of Red Rock. No sign of the small, mud-brick hovels, or the Comm Building.

It took him a moment to realize he'd ended up on the far side of the eastern wall. Darius wanted to turn and explore the tunnel's other direction, but if he stayed too long, his exploration might run until daylight.

If he were caught, or missed, he might never see what was on the other side of this new tunnel.

Eventually, his good sense won out, and Darius snuffed out his light and snuck out into the moonlight, intent on getting back to his colony before daybreak.

Chapter 30: Neena

A CRUNCHING NOISE ECHOED FROM SOMEWHERE below. Neena startled, ripped from her dozing. Her memories came back to her as she balanced on the rocky ledge, searching the darkened desert. Kai sat up slowly beside her. The twin moons cast a pale glow over the landscape, illuminating the outlines of some of the dunes. Neena guessed it was close to morning, but not close enough.

More crunching.

Whatever was below them was bigger than a bird.

Slowly, Neena scooted closer to the edge, peering down toward the holes. A few shadows moved between them, munching quietly. Neena listened as they tore and chewed on the carcass.

Occasionally, a growl floated up to where they perched. *Wolves.*

Neena steeled herself on the ledge. Listening to the noises below, she felt a fear she hadn't had in many years. All at once, she was thirteen and hunting with her father again, huddled in a cave, clutching the small spear she'd had back then and listening to a wolf pack sharing their kill outside. She and her father's small fire had petered out, taking away the protection of smoke, so that all they could do was wait and hide. She'd clutched Dad and listened to the animals growl, crunch, and shift in the dark, certain that the wolves would come for them next. That night had been sleepless, like too many others in those early hunting days.

Feeling the weight of that memory, Neena held on to her knife. Kai kept close, giving her a measure of comfort. After a long while, the wolves slunk off into the night, finished with their scraps. She watched their shadows merge with the darkness.

If only she had a spear.

Maybe she could've gotten lucky and killed one of them for food.

Neena stayed awake until rays of sunlight crept over the eastern horizon, watching for the wolves. They didn't return. Peering over the ledge, she spotted the remains of the fawn. What had once been recognizable was now a pile of blood and fur. Small ribs protruded from the last of the fawn's flesh; the sand was stained red.

As unappetizing as the fawn had been, the rest of their makeshift meal was gone.

Neena saw no new holes. A small reassurance, she thought, after another night with not enough sleep. Too many of those were already taking their toll. Neena felt the fatigue in her muscles, which were sore from so much travel, and in her eyes, which were harder to keep open after several nights of mostly dozing. Blinking through her dizziness, she reached for her flask and nursed the last of her water, while Kai also drank.

They stood, stretching out their legs under a sun that was slowly rising.

"We should get off this ledge before the daytime heat bakes us," Neena suggested.

"Of course." Kai chewed his lip, looking down at the carcass. Thinking on something, he said, "It isn't often that I see a pack of wolves."

"There are a few packs around here, but usually, they

stay clear of us," Neena told him. "Of course, food has been getting harder to find." A thought she'd had the night before came back to her. "If we come across any wood, perhaps we should fashion some spears today."

"Probably a good idea," Kai said.

Returning to the ledge, they maneuvered their way down, a little more familiar with the climb now.

Reaching the stream without incident, they drank wordlessly, replenishing their flasks. Neena put her hands over her eyes to ward off some of the sun's emerging glare. Having made the decision to return to her colony the night before, Neena had one less worry. She could already feel the tug of her brothers, pulling her toward Red Rock. Now, they just needed to make it there alive.

"How long do we have left to travel?" Kai asked, following her gaze.

"If we can make it without incident, we should be to Red Rock by late morning tomorrow, with only another night in the desert," Neena said. Saying those words gave her a small dose of relief.

"What else is between here and your colony?" Kai asked.

"There is a place to get water a ways from here. We should have enough water to reach it."

"A stream?"

"A tree with large roots," Neena clarified. "Usually I tap the base and find some water." She looked down at her flasks. Normally, her extra flask kept her insulated against dehydration, but sharing with Kai had been a stretch. They'd have to make do.

"What is the terrain like?" Kai asked.

Neena thought on that. "The ground gets a little firmer, with more rugged hills than dunes. We'll have to travel through desert for about a dozen klicks to get to it." As she spoke the words, she found herself wishing the terrain would help, but she knew only rock was safe.

"Are there any more caves up ahead, or rock formations that will give us shelter like the ones where we've stayed?" Kai asked.

"There is a long, wide rock that forms an alcove, which we should reach before nightfall," Neena said. "It's usually where I stay, on the way back to my colony."

"That sounds like a place toward which to head," Kai agreed. "At the very least, we'll be out of the sand. We both know how tiring the tug of the desert can be on weary feet."

Neena agreed.

With the decision made, they made their way south over the windswept desert, away from the carcass, the holes, and the rock formation. Neena was grateful to gain some distance between places that were now laced with bad memories. The thought struck her that she might never see them again.

It seemed as if Neena's old life had been swept away. Or maybe it was the urgency of returning to Red Rock, which seemed to take away all thoughts of the future.

They resumed their pace from the day before, walking in the same quiet pattern that kept them safe. A few soaring birds gave them a measure of comfort. When they were about level with the dune where they'd seen the spray of sand, Neena looked over, noticing several giant holes in the distance. This time, she saw no carcass.

"Whatever that animal was, I hope it received a quick death," Kai whispered grimly.

Neena swallowed the lump in her throat, refraining from more conversation. They walked under the burgeoning sun, past more uneven, sloped dunes, until the heat became oppressive. Having traveled with Kai a little longer now, Neena was acquainted with his mannerisms. When he worried, he scratched his chin. When he was more relaxed, he walked with his hands at his sides, but he never stopped scanning the desert. *Definitely a hunter*, she thought.

Watching him, more questions came to her.

"What is it like at your colony?" she asked him.

"We live in an oasis, around a small lake, as I mentioned," Kai said. "Our houses are built in an area of more compact soil, though we get plenty of sand blowing in around us."

"Do you have wood there?"

"We have to travel for it," Kai said.

"Like everything else, wood is scarce," Neena said knowingly. Thinking back to some of the many stories she'd heard as a child, about buildings like the Comm Building, she asked, "What are your buildings made of?"

"Stone, mostly," Kai explained.

"You don't use mud brick?"

"More and more people are moving away from mud brick, as their old houses crumble. They think it might help the with the Abomination attacks."

Neena nodded. She understood his concern. "Do you have any that are made of enormous, smooth stone?"

Kai seemed confused. "Large pieces from the desert, you mean?"

"Buildings built with tools we no longer have," Neena said.

"Tools from Earth, you mean," Kai said, his voice filling with the same wonder that had driven her questions.

Neena nodded. She stared at Kai, surprised to hear the answer at which she'd hinted, but wasn't sure he'd understand. It was strange hearing the same term coming from the lips of a stranger. "It sounds as if you have the same stories as us."

"It is believed that everyone on Earth is dead. Is that what you've heard?" Kai asked.

Neena nodded. Speaking of the mysterious place always gave her a sense of awe. "A few people think that we were stranded, generations ago. Some say that our home planet lost the resources to get to us here. Some say a large catastrophe happened that made it impossible for them to reach us again."

"It sounds as if your people are no closer to an answer than mine," Kai said, with a sigh. "How long have your people been here?"

"Our people were sent here on a mining mission a few generations ago," Neena said. "It was to last a few years, perhaps longer. I don't think we were meant to stay forever."

Kai thought on that. "I believe we were sent to colonize, though the stories differ. In any case, I do not think either of us will get off this planet."

"Unfortunately, true," Neena said. Recalling her original question, she said, "It sounds as if you know about the type of stone to which I'm referring."

"We don't have any buildings like that, but I know what you are describing," Kai agreed, waving a vague hand across the desert. "About two generations ago, our people moved from another place, farther away, with structures said to be from Earth. The hunting had gotten so bad that our ancestors were forced to head for a new area. Of course, the buildings were too large to move, but a few pieces from the original settlement have found their way into our homes."

"How far is that place from your colony?" Neena asked.

"Many days north from New Canaan, wherever it is," Kai said, relaying what was clearly an old story. "They say lots of people died during that move. It is a journey that no one has dared to make since. What food existed there is long gone." Kai thought on it with a shrug. "Even if there were food and we wanted to journey back, with the Abomination in the desert, making that much vibration would be suicide."

Neena opened and closed her mouth to too many questions. "I can't believe the places you describe exist."

"And I can't believe we have come across each other," Kai said. "Meeting you makes me wonder if other people exist."

Neena nodded as she thought about that. "They do. At least, I think they do."

"What do you mean?"

"Years ago, when I was a child, it was said that some people visited our colony," Neena explained. "It has been enough years that it has almost become a rumor. But I remember some of the whispers of our people, as the story was passed among us. Our leaders were said to have met with them."

"It couldn't have been us," Kai said. "Our leaders would have told us about it."

"Exactly what I was thinking," Neena said. "But even if our people haven't met, I think your theory must be right about others, especially when I reconsider those rumors."

Kai nodded. "That is incredible to think about."

"What do you call this planet?" Neena asked.

"Ravar."

"We have the same term, then," Neena affirmed. "That makes me believe the stories we've heard from our ancestors were true."

Turning an earlier question on her, Kai asked, "Those buildings made with the material you described before. Do you have them?"

"We have one," Neena said. "It is called the Comm Building. Our leaders live there, along with some of the people who look after us."

Wonder filled Kai's eyes. "The Comm Building. I would like to see it."

"You will, once we reach Red Rock," Neena said. "It is in the center of our colony. Of course, we will have to get there, first."

Kai nodded. "For more than one reason, I hope that we do."

Chapter 31: Raj

AJ, SAMEL, AND HELGID WALKED with their heads
bowed, exiting a row of dirty, mud brick houses
and merging onto the main pathway. All around
them, men, women, and children traveled the smaller alleys,
converging into a single procession. The men looked at each
other with sullen, commiserating expressions. The women
walked with their heads down, herding their children, or
keeping the younger ones quiet. Their slow trudge reminded
Raj of the flow of the river toward which they headed — a
single mass, pouring steadily in the direction of the bridge.

Filing onto the main path, Raj, Helgid, and Samel
fell into a row with several others, slowing their pace to
accommodate new people. A boy a year or two younger
than Samel tugged on his mother's arm, resisting the flow of
the crowd. A few of the elderly colonists coughed into their
shawls, not used to the exertion, or a journey that took them
so far from their homes. All were expected to come, unless
they were gravely ill.

Samel walked quietly, mirroring the expressions of
those around him. Every once in a while, he snuck a glance
at Raj. During the last procession, Samel had whispered
several questions, earning disapproving looks from those
around them.

Today, he behaved as expected.

Samel was learning.

Deep in the distance, the first of the colonists in line

reached the ten-foot-wide wooden bridge, making room for one another as they shuffled into rows, eventually spilling off the other side and reforming. Raj looked for Bailey and his friends in the line, but he didn't see any of them in the dense crowd.

With no sight of them since yesterday, he allowed a hope to grow: perhaps they'd heeded the Watcher's warning, and would leave him and Samel alone.

The procession continued past the rows of Green Crops on the other side of the bridge, and curved, headed toward the far end of the western rock formation in a slow, deliberate procession.

Raj's hand moved to his right pocket, where he kept the strange metal gift. His thoughts drifted to Adriana.

He looked around again, but he didn't see anyone who fit the brief memory he had of her. He had thought of her often last night before sleep, as he'd rolled the strange gift in his hand in the dark. The metal keepsake was as unexpected as their chance encounter. Try as he might, he couldn't solidify Adriana's appearance in his mind, having only seen her the day her grandmother died.

Hopefully, he'd recognize her at the ceremony.

Soon Raj, Helgid, and Samel passed over the wooden bridge, their boots clopping on the wooden planks. Raj looked over the four-foot-high railing to the river. Every so often, on a normal day, one of the younger children disobeyed a parent's warning, climbed, and lost their balance. Most of the time, those children were fished from the slow-moving river before they drowned, but every once in a while, a tragic accident occurred. Thankfully, Samel knew better than to horse around.

Crossing the bridge, they passed the Green Crops on either side, reaching a patch of open desert that ran between the last parts of the cliffs.

Not for the first time, Raj pictured his father alone in

the desert, wandering farther and farther away from the colony. His father was never far from his mind, every time he attended a ceremony. And neither was his mother.

Raj looked up at the highest western cliffs, toward which the line veered. A few of The Watchers stood, silhouetted by the sun, keeping track of the people below, or looking out for storms. Raj didn't need to look to know that some of The Watchers stood on the eastern cliffs, as well.

The crowd rounded the western cliffs, following the path to the other side.

The Watchers disappeared from sight.

An open landscape spanned as far as the eye could see. The path on which they traveled ran parallel to the cliffs, but beyond, several hundred feet were dotted with rocks and stones, spanning the width of the other side of the rock formation and eventually seguing to desert.

The graveyard.

Staring at the graveyard, Raj saw sections.

The freshest graves — those that hadn't been claimed by the desert — were at the far end of the graveyard, mostly unburied by the shifting sands. The slightly older graves were in the middle, reduced to tips of stones. And the oldest were mostly invisible.

About halfway back, in the middle section, was the empty grave that marked Raj's father, along with the full one that marked his mother. He scanned the hundreds of stones, as if he might find them, but he was too far back to see.

It had been too long since he visited them on his own.

He made a mental note to visit them soon.

The line kept going until the colonists reached the western edge of the graveyard, where the freshest graves were located.

A group of two-dozen men stood at the threshold of three newly dug holes. Next to them, three bodies lay wrapped in sheets, ready for burial. As the line reached the waiting men, the bereaved relatives broke from the crowd and lined up — the men in front, the women behind, so their crying could not be heard over the speech to come. Next, the other colonists filed into spectating rows, where they could watch the ceremony.

Raj searched for Adriana among the bereaved. He noticed a few young women that fit her description, but it was impossible to tell for certain, because most wore shawls over their faces.

Raj, Helgid, and Samel merged into one of the long rows of colonists facing the graves, settling about ten rows from the front. When the last sounds of crunching boots stopped, the desert quieted and they waited for the ceremony to begin.

All eyes turned to a man who stepped a few paces in front of the two dozen important men. Raj and Samel shifted, looking through the rows of the crowd, so that they could see the colony leader.

Gideon's stern expression did not change as he scanned the crowd. Looking over his shoulder, he nodded at his Heads of Colony, and his Watchers, before speaking. His austere voice carried over the crowd.

"The heavens have claimed the lives of three more of us, but they are not lost," Gideon began, loud enough to be heard by all in the desert quiet. "The winds that took them from our colony will carry them upward and on to better things, to a place where food is plentiful, to a place where the elements cannot harm them. The whispered words of our ancestors will comfort them as they move from this life to the next."

A few heads bowed. A few women shed quiet tears.

"The heavens will guard these stones, so that our deceased are never alone. They will not be forgotten." A subtle breeze blew, lifting the hair of the bereaved women, some of whom had removed their shawls to blot their faces. "We will remember them by the lives they led, and the people they touched."

The crowd alternated its focus between Gideon and the wrapped, lifeless bodies. Raj noticed a few children in the front row shifting from foot to foot. He looked over at Samel, thinking he might have to scold him, but Samel stood quietly and rigidly. Sensing Raj's eyes, he looked over and nodded.

Another of The Heads of Colony, Wyatt, stepped forward from the important men. Normally, the tall, skinny man reserved his voice for passing out rations or giving directions to The Watchers who carried out Gideon's projects. Today, it served another purpose. Tilting his head up to the sky as if he sought wisdom from the sun or the twin moons, Wyatt spoke.

"The heavens have a purpose for taking our loved ones, greater than any of our individual comprehension. We honor our loved ones, as painful as their passing might be, by carrying on their hard work. We persevere in their memory." Wyatt beckoned to the three bodies. "We will remember them by carrying on in their name. That is their legacy."

Listening to Wyatt, Raj felt a pit in his stomach. Raj barely recalled his mother's funeral, but he recalled his father's with clarity. The crowd had proceeded in the same march. The men had watched solemnly. Children had clung to their parents, listening. But those speeches sounded different, without a body to bury.

Dad had only an empty grave to mark his remains, and few relatives to remember him. He had no whispers from ancestors to take him to the sky. His body had long rotted in the desert, food for the few animals clinging to life out there. Or maybe he was buried, like the oldest graves.

Neena had looked for him, but she hadn't found him.

Or, at least, that was what she told Raj, although sometimes he suspected she was holding something back.

He listened as Wyatt concluded his speech and stepped back into line, and The Watchers moved forward to start the burials. Scanning the three wrapped sheets, Raj wondered which was the woman he'd helped pull from that collapsed house.

He didn't have to guess for long.

One of the bereaved — a girl — uncovered her face, letting out a long wail as she moved past the others, kneeling at the first grave's edge. Raj recognized her long, dark hair and her mannerisms. She brushed away tears with slender hands as she spoke quiet words and The Watchers lowered the first body, before she moved back to embrace her relatives, all of whom listened intently for the rest of the ceremony.

That must be Adriana, he thought.

Chapter 32: Darius

DARIUS SCURRIED THROUGH THE COLONY with his cane. During the ceremony, he had made sure to keep his distance from the others, including Elmer, out of a cautious fear that someone might suspect something.

Now, he headed to his friend's house.

He couldn't get his mind off of what he'd seen in the caves. He needed to talk with Elmer in private.

Walking up to the old, faded house he'd visited the day before, Darius found Elmer returning.

"Elmer!" he called, with enough vigor to make the man turn from the doorway.

Elmer's good eye lit up as he saw his friend. "Darius!"

"Can I come in?" Darius looked on either side of him. Everyone else was preoccupied with returning home, tending to their children, or heading off to morning chores. A handful—the Crop Tenders who lived close by—headed off to work detail.

"Sure," Elmer said, leading his friend inside.

Darius walked into the familiar hovel. Unlike Darius's house, which was filled with scraps of metal and weapons to be fixed, Elmer's house was relatively clean. The house contained only cookware, a few piles of clothing, and a tidy hearth. Darius's eyes flicked to the long, brown shawl hanging on the wall, which had belonged to Elmer's dead wife. He felt a tug of sympathy.

"I'll shut the door," Elmer said, waiting until Darius

was inside before he closed it. Without the commotion of the alleys to distract them, he asked in a whisper, "How did it go last night?"

Darius looked behind him. He still couldn't convince himself that a shadow hadn't followed him from the cave's bowels, watching him scurry through the streets, to his house, and to the ceremony. *And here.* Maybe someone had noticed him hurrying back with his bag and unloading it. Maybe a group of Watchers waited outside to bring him to Gideon and punish him.

Keeping his voice low, he said, "I found something in the tunnels."

"What did you find?" Elmer's face grew serious as he shuffled closer.

"I was in the eastern section, past the first few intersections, and through the cave broken down by the old miners," Darius started, realizing he rambled about a place where Elmer had never been. To his credit, Elmer didn't question him. "I was halfway down that tunnel when I frightened a fox, and it ran into a hole in the wall."

"A den," Elmer assumed.

"That's what I thought, at first," Darius said, keeping his voice hushed as he got to the crux of the discovery. "Until I saw the place where it disappeared. The fox scooted into a hole in the wall, covered by rocks. I uncovered them and found a passage leading to a tunnel I've never seen."

Elmer leaned forward, listening intently.

"Even I'm not foolish enough to think there are places I haven't discovered," Darius clarified, "but there was something about this passage that made it even more intriguing." Darius paused, making sure he had the full attention of his friend's good eye. "Akron's mark was on the wall, right near it."

Wonder filled Elmer's face, as he remembered, "A triangle."

Darius nodded.

"Did you find anything else?" Elmer asked.

Darius shook his head. "I looked around a while, following the new tunnel to its end, until I reached an exit. By that time, it was late enough that I had to get back."

"You didn't want to be caught," Elmer said, knowingly.

"I still have one more side to explore," Darius told him. "I have no idea what is on the other end, or how many other passages it might reveal."

"At least you will have a place on which to focus, when you return," Elmer said.

"Maybe tonight," Darius said.

"Tonight?" Elmer seemed surprised. "That is risky. Usually you space out your visits, Darius."

"I think this is worth the risk," Darius said, unable to get his mind off of Akron. "I can't stop thinking about that tunnel, Elmer. I need to see what is in it."

Chapter 33: Neena

SLOWLY, THE DESERT UNDERNEATH NEENA'S and Kai's boots gave way to more solid terrain. Rocks of various sizes littered the ground as far as the eye could see, with wispy shrubs reaching for sunlight in between. In a few spots, hills jutted out from the brown earth, covered with larger rocks, and a few coarse plants made of a sickly green. A smattering of sand covered the landscape, carried by the storm, or the daily winds.

Neena welcomed the easier travel, as they stepped from the sand to firmer ground.

But she had a new fear, too.

In the sand, they knew what to expect. Here, a single noise on the slightly harder ground might lure the hungry beast. She picked a path between rocks, avoiding noisy clomps that might give them away, walking heel to toe, as she had done in the desert. They walked for some time, under a sun that grew hotter.

Neena chose a path between two familiar hills, where sparse weeds shot up from the sides. She studied the ground for cracks or holes—anything that would indicate that the creature had gotten ahead of them—but she saw none. Reaching up, she dabbed away some sweat with her shawl.

"Over there," Kai said, pointing, as they passed the two hills and found another. A tall, recognizable tree jutted out from the new hill's base. "Is that the tree?"

"Yes, that's the warden's root, of which I spoke," Neena said.

Kai looked at her with a quizzical expression. "You mean a sandalwood?"

"We must call it different things," she said. They had similarities, but of course they had differences.

"No matter what you call it, we should probably fill our flasks," Kai suggested.

Neena nodded. They veered from their path, skirting more boot-sized rocks and getting closer to the broadleaf tree. The warden's root rose several feet before expanding into a multitude of branches, jutting out at different angles. Round, green leaves stuck off of the ends of those limbs, providing some welcome color in the mostly desolate landscape. More than once, Neena had run into other hunters in the area, collecting liquid from the tree's base.

She saw no one now.

A strange, ominous feeling took hold of her: for a brief moment, it felt as if she and Kai were the only people left on Ravar, and everyone else had vanished. Shaking off the thought, she walked softly and looked left and right, until she reached the warden's root, one of the few things in this area that retained enough water to be worth tapping. Unslinging her bag, she pulled out a small wedge that she had fashioned—a tiny, hollowed-out stick that allowed water to pass through to her flask from trees such as this.

She knelt and quietly dug near the tree's base with her knife, working around a few old notches. Kai looked as if he wanted to help, but with only one blade between them, he waited. After tapping the tree and putting in her wedge, she watched water drip into her flask, doing the same with Kai's. The process was slow, but soon she had replenished most of what they drank.

"We'll have to ration the water, of course," she said.

Kai nodded.

Neena remained underneath the thin shade of the tree for a moment, cooling off, while Kai took small sips from his replenished flask.

"Look over there," he said, spotting something on the hill.

Neena followed his gaze.

Walking up the hill to retrieve a broken limb, he said, "One of the branches fell from the tree. The wood is dry. Maybe we can make those spears we talked about this morning."

"Can I see it?"

He handed the branch to Neena, who gauged its thickness. "We won't be able to fire dry them, but I think you have a good idea." The prospect of having something other than a knife to fill her hands was a welcome thought.

"We'll have to work quietly, of course," Kai warned, looking around the landscape. "And quickly. Perhaps we can fashion them at the top of the hill, where we'll have a better view of our surroundings."

With an agreement reached, they ascended the small climb, gaining a better view of the landscape. Deep in the north, Neena saw the quashed dunes of the desert they'd left behind. To the south she saw more of the same hard ground. Spotting nothing of concern, she knelt and clutched the branch, cutting it in half and starting on the first of the spears. She carved a tip sharp enough to jab, to hunt. Kai watched her with respect.

"I'll admit, I haven't seen many women performing the task."

"Not many women know how," Neena said with a shrug. "But it is a necessary skill."

"Of course."

It took her a while, whittling at the wood, but eventually she fashioned a crude point at the end, hefting the stick in her hands. The spear wasn't as comfortable or as sleek as her old one, but it would ward off an animal, if they needed. Finished with the weapon, she took a practice heave. Noticing Kai's gaze, she handed it to him.

He hefted it, while Neena carved another.

"This is a lot sharper than the stick I carried," Kai said gratefully.

When she had finished, she tucked away her knife and held up the second spear. It felt as if too much time had passed without one. With weapons to fill their hands and some water in their flasks, they continued down the hill and headed south.

Chapter 34: Raj

RAJ STOOD OUTSIDE OF HELGID'S house, turning the strange metal keepsake in his hand.

The grieving girl at the ceremony had to be Adriana.

Raj didn't want to bother her. She had just lost someone. But he did want to thank her.

Pondering that for a moment, he decided that he would find her house, speak to her, and see how it went. If she asked him to leave, or seemed upset at his presence, he would say a quick word of condolence and go.

Heading past a few houses, he waved at a few of Helgid's neighbors, who busied themselves with chores. Most liked Raj, but they kept their distance, knowing they didn't have enough food to feed him. Occasionally, he felt resentful about their strange behavior, but not today.

The sun felt good on his skin as Raj retraced his steps down a handful of alleys, returning the piece of metal carefully to his pocket. He wondered how long the poor, dead woman had owned the piece, or where it came from. He envisioned the strange object traveling through the heavens on some strange craft, over distances he couldn't imagine. Could it be that old? Helgid had said the girl didn't know much about it, but she certainly knew more than Raj. Maybe if he asked more questions, she would remember something.

Of course, he didn't know how long he'd stay, or if he'd even speak to her at all.

He walked until he found the alley where he'd tried helping the dead woman a few days ago. A large, vacant space sat between two houses, marking where her house had been. Only a few small piles of sand remained. It appeared The Watchers had already finished cleaning up the wreckage.

Looking at the area, he relived the memory of the pale, sand-covered woman for a moment.

Eventually, the weight of the object in his pocket made him recall why he had come, and his gaze wandered to the houses on either side of the vacant spot. Both doors were closed. Where did the girl live? A man on the opposite side of the alley stood at a doorway, looking at him. Raj suddenly felt conspicuous. The last thing he needed was to look like he was a boy in search of trouble.

Or a thief.

Looking at the closed doors, he wasn't sure on which door he should knock.

He was about to make a choice when the door to the left-hand house opened and a middle-aged woman with a gray bun on her head walked out, carrying a pot in her hand. She emptied some of the extra water next to her doorway. Finishing her chore, she looked up and spotted him. Raj approached tentatively, putting on an innocuous expression and hoping she wouldn't shoo him away.

"Do you know where I can find Adriana?" he asked.

The woman watched him for a second, gauging his intentions. After a pause, she answered. "She lives in the house over there." Raj followed her pointing finger to the house on the other side of the empty rubble.

Before he could ask another question, the door opened and the girl he had seen at the ceremony walked out, smoothing her shirt and pants. Raj had a moment to take her in before she noticed him. It was hard to reconcile the crying girl at the ceremony with the calm person in front of him, or the wailing one he'd seen outside her grandmother's house.

Adriana's dark hair fell to her shoulders. Her cheeks were thin, her nose of perfect proportion. Her eyes were blue. She looked about a year or two younger than Neena. He was within a few feet when she looked over.

A small smile overtook the sadness on her face, as she called, "It's you."

Raj walked to meet her. Parroting the words The Heads of Colony told all of them, he said, "I'm sorry for what happened to your grandmother. I hope she finds her peace in the heavens."

An empty silence filled the air as they appraised one another, and Raj felt the urge to leave. Now that he was here, his idea to ask her more questions felt silly.

"I appreciate what you tried to do for her," Adriana said. "I will certainly miss her."

Feeling a sheepishness he wasn't used to, Raj said, "I got the gift you left for me." He dug it out of his pocket, as if to prove he was the same person. "Here it is." He blushed as he fought back feelings he hadn't expected. Hoping to distract from his embarrassment, he held the object higher so they both had something to focus on.

If Adriana noticed his discomfort, she didn't let on. Her smile grew as she saw the object in his hand, and looked back at him. "I'm glad you received it."

"You didn't have to give it to me," Raj said. "I was happy to help."

"You earned it." Adriana said with a firm nod. "My grandmother would be happy you have it." Sadness tugged at the corners of her lips.

Once again, Raj felt self-conscious.

Before he could excuse himself, Adriana said, "Would you like to come inside for some tea?"

Raj looked over his shoulder, as if someone might be

expecting him, but of course they weren't. Before he could second-guess his decision, he said, "Sure. I would like that."

Adriana's house was in better shape than some of the surrounding houses, or at least, it looked that way, from the inside. Unlike most of the hovels Raj visited, he saw only a few obvious patches on the walls. The place was tidy and clean, with the cookware placed on a stone shelf on one of the far walls. A few piles of clothes and blankets sat neatly in another corner. It looked as if someone lived here, other than her.

Answering his unspoken question, Adriana said, "My parents are down by the river. They are dividing up a few things we rescued from Nana's house with some of our relatives."

"I see," said Raj.

Some guilt crossed her face as she said, "We were lucky in this last storm. We didn't sustain much damage, unlike Nana." Adriana sighed. "More than once, we asked her to stay with us. Nana's house was one of the older ones. We did what we could to fix it, but she was stubborn. She wouldn't leave. And she wouldn't let us rebuild it."

Raj nodded. He knew how the elderly could be attached to tradition.

"I used to have tea with her every morning," Adriana said, putting a kettle over the fire. "It has been strange to wake up the past few days, without her."

Raj nodded. He knew the pain of losing his mother and father, and with Neena gone much of the time, he often felt alone.

"I am speaking as if I am the only one who has lost someone," Adriana said. "I'm sorry. I know you have lost people, too."

Raj was confused, before he figured something out.

"I spoke with Helgid a while yesterday," Adriana explained. "She told me you, your brother, and sister live alone."

Raj lowered his head, as an unexpected emotion rose to the surface. "My parents have been gone a while."

"It sounds as if you are lucky to have Helgid."

"She is great," Raj said, without hesitation.

"I could tell that," Adriana said. "She spoke fondly of you, Samel, and your sister Neena."

"Neena is out hunting," Raj said. Revealing a fear, he added, "I'm worried she might've been caught in the sandstorm, but she is savvy. I'm sure she will be home soon."

"It is rare to find a woman who can hunt to provide," Adriana said. "She sounds special."

"She is."

"I'm sure she'll be back soon," Adriana reassured him.

She smiled as she poured him a cup of tea, and Raj blew on the top to cool it. For the first time in a while, he felt a sense of calm. Adriana was a stranger to him, and yet, it felt like he had known her for longer than a chance meeting. And she didn't judge him, like too many others did.

Some of the initial questions he'd thought of came back to him.

Pulling out the object from his pocket again, Raj asked, "Do you mind if I ask some questions about it?"

"Sure. I expected you might come." Adriana smiled. "I will answer what I can."

"What does it do?"

"No one in our family was quite sure what it did, or used to do, but Nana insisted on preserving it over the years. She told me it was passed down through the generations." Adriana sighed as she reflected. "Even when times grew tough, they did not trade it, or melt it down. Eventually, she gave it to me."

"It is fascinating," Raj said.

"I thought so, too," Adriana said. "Like you, I wish I knew what it did, but I suspect we will never know."

"How long have you had it?"

"About ten years," Adriana said. "I am not sure why, but it gives me a strange comfort."

Raj felt a pang of guilt as he stared at the object. "Why did you give it to me?"

"It felt right," Adriana said emphatically. "I think Nana would've wanted me to."

"You should take it back," he said, holding it out in his palm. "Surely you will want it, to remember her."

Adriana refused the offer. Instead, she made a fist and clutched it to her chest. "Nana is always in here. Wherever she is, I'm sure she approves of my giving it to you."

"Thank you," Raj said, and he meant it. He stared at the object with an emotion he wasn't used to feeling. Looking at the object made him recall similar, sentimental items, like one that his sister owned. "My sister carries my father's spear. It was one of his few possessions. Whenever I see it, I think of him."

Adriana smiled. "Was he a good hunter?"

"He was," Raj said, with more than a little pride. "He taught my sister. He was supposed to teach me, too, before..." His words trailed off and he looked down, ashamed.

Sympathy crossed Adriana's face. She set down her tea, touching his arm. "What happened?"

"He got sick." Raj stuck his chin up, staving off his emotion. "I watched his body grow from strong to brittle. He left so that we wouldn't have to take care of him, and so that we could keep on living."

"He sounds brave," Adriana affirmed, squeezing Raj's arm. "I can tell by the way you speak of him."

"The bravest," Raj said, repeating what Neena always

told them. "He looked after us for a handful of years, after my mother died giving birth to Samel."

Letting go of his arm, Adriana looked to the ceiling. "Perhaps both of your parents are watching us now, with Nana. I think they would be happy we have met."

A sad smile crossed Raj's face. "I think so, too."

With their tea cooled, they each took long sips. The drink warmed Raj's stomach, even though the desert was quickly heating up. They chatted for a while, until their conversation segued to a comfortable silence.

After finishing their tea, Adriana collected the cups and told him, "Feel free to come by any time, Raj."

"I will."

Chapter 35: Neena

THE LANDSCAPE — EASIER TO NAVIGATE WHEN they first entered it — was now ridden with obstacles. Each step Neena and Kai took came with the fear of a foot sliding too harshly on a plethora of rocks. Normally, a twisted ankle would've slowed Neena's pace notably, but now they had greater threats. They conversed little as they contended with the rockier path, concentrating on each footfall. A few times, they stopped to tap smaller trees for their water, getting enough of a drip to keep them hydrated. The sun had turned a hot day into a sweltering one. Kai wiped his brow more than she had noticed earlier.

Eventually, they reached an area of compacted ground, with fewer pitfalls.

Kai seemed lost in thought.

"You seem as if you are thinking about something," Neena noticed, as she returned her flask to her belt from a drink.

"I was wondering about the years we've lived side by side, without knowing about each other," Kai said. "And that reminded me of something you said earlier."

"What?" Neena asked.

"You told me that your people often wander into the desert when they are ill, before they die," he said. "That makes me surprised that we have never met any of them."

"Our people find them," Neena explained. "Most of the ill go off without their belongings, leaving their personal items to their relatives. They bring none of their possessions, so that their death is certain. We recover most of the bodies and bring them back for burial."

Kai nodded.

Speaking of the dead brought some emotions to the surface that Neena had never had a real chance to process. One particular memory weighed on Neena as she walked. She concentrated on her footsteps, until some of her memories came out into words.

"I remember the day I found my father," she recalled, not realizing that she was going to speak until the words spilled out. "It was several weeks after he left."

Kai looked over sympathetically, waiting for her to explain.

"My father was a spiritual man," she continued. "He believed in the powers of our ancestors, and the heavens. And so I respected his wishes and did not go after him, until later." She paused a moment, making sure she explained her tradition properly. "If I were to find him before he died, he might not make it to the heavens."

"I understand."

"In the days after he left, my brothers kept asking questions. They were young, and they didn't understand our tradition. Or maybe they didn't want to. They asked me to go after him right away. A few times, I had to stop my oldest brother from leaving on his own. Eventually, I promised Raj that I would search for him when I hunted. I remember the looks on my brothers' faces as I said goodbye for my first hunt. They hoped for a miracle that I knew I wouldn't be able to give them. But I had no choice except to leave. We needed food. It was my first time, going out without my father."

"You were the provider."

Neena nodded. "I was all we had." She sighed, looking into the sky a moment, before continuing her story. "It was strange, walking through the desert without my father.

I was used to talking with him, asking questions. It felt as if he should be by my side, even though he wasn't, or that maybe I would find him somewhere, waiting. A part of me wondered if maybe our ancestors performed some miracle and took away his sickness." Neena sighed. "It was a childish hope that even I didn't believe, but my brothers' faith was infectious."

Kai nodded.

"I searched for a while without finding him. I scoured the desert, and some of the caves and old fires near where we stayed, with his spear in my hand. Eventually, I came across a circle of rocks about a half day outside of our colony. As soon as I approached, I realized I would find him there. It was the first place we stopped, on our first hunt. It was the place where he took my shoulders, held my eye, and told me that I needed to be strong, if anything were to happen to him. It was the place where he taught me how to hold my spear."

"He sent you a sign, even in his death."

"He did," Neena said, quickly blotting away a tear. "His body was there, leaning against a rock. He wanted me to find him, so that I would remember our talk, years ago. I'll never forget that conversation. When I close my eyes, I can still see his face, and I can hear the things he taught me. They guide me on every hunt. And his spear reminded me of him. Of course, now that is gone."

"I am sorry."

"You do not have to be sorry." Neena composed herself. "He was loved, and he was buried. Sometimes, that is all we can hope for in this life."

They walked further, watching their feet, while Kai allowed her some respectful silence. "How did your brothers react when you brought him back?"

"I never brought him back," Neena said, lowering her head as she made an admission. "I was alone, with no one with me to help with his body. And so I buried my father in the desert, underneath those stones, where no one would find him. In some way, I wanted to preserve my brothers' hope." She tightened her grip on the spear. "I am not sure if that was the right thing to do."

"You did what you thought was best," Kai said.

"It was the decision I made at the time." Neena gazed into the clear sky. "Perhaps one day I will tell my brothers the truth. I think Raj suspects that there is something I haven't told him. But hopefully, for now, they will carry him in their hearts."

Chapter 36: Gideon

"GIDEON!"

Gideon stared past the clustered colonists on the main pathway, searching for the source of the shout. Beside him, Wyatt tensed as he reached for his knife. All around them, men and women filled the streets and the areas around the mud brick houses. A few mothers hurried their children along as they saw two of the leaders coming, trying to keep occupied.

"Gideon!" the cry came again.

More commotion rose above the noise.

Seeing something, mothers pulled their children from harm's way.

Gideon tensed as more people recognized something was happening and scattered. A hundred feet away, Thorne and two of his Watchers pulled a gaunt, flailing man up the path. Relaxing slightly, Gideon waited for the men to get close, appraising a man he didn't recognize.

Spotting Gideon and Wyatt, Thorne gave the man a tug. "Let's go."

More people emerged from their homes, stopping to gawk, or waiting for whatever came next. The air was silent, save the man's desperate cries. Sensing the riveted eyes of a growing crowd, Gideon arched his back.

Projecting his voice so that everyone in the crowd swiveled to listen, he asked, "What's going on?"

The man in the Watcher's grasp stopped yelling. He opened his mouth to answer, but fear caught his tongue.

Cutting in, Thorne held up a bulging sack. "We caught him stealing from one of the pushcarts in the storehouses. He waited for a moment we weren't looking, and made off with some vegetables before we could distribute them."

"Is that true?" Gideon demanded, meeting the man's fearful eyes.

No answer.

"Open the bag," Gideon said.

Thorne undid the bag and opened it, revealing a sack full of vegetables and roots. Some were green, while others were wilted, their stems snapped.

Damaged crops.

The man opened and closed his mouth, reaching for an argument, too late.

There was no disputing the damning evidence.

"What should we do with him?" Thorne asked, snapping the bag shut with triumphant finality.

Gideon looked at the man, noticing a few long, bloody scrapes on his cheeks. The Watchers had undoubtedly tackled him. He looked sideways, as if he might find more conspirators in the crowd, but the rest were silent. "Take him to the annex. Throw him in a cell. Keep him there as long as I see fit."

Chapter 37: Darius

ARIUS PACED AROUND HIS SMALL hovel. For a while after returning home, he'd worked on one of the neighbor's spears, but too many swirling thoughts made it impossible to focus.

Ever since leaving that strange cave, he'd reviewed his exploration in his head, wondering whether he might've missed something. He was confident he'd been thorough. He'd canvassed the tunnels as well as he was able, shining his light into crevices, searching for more passages like the one he'd found, but he'd found only miner's marks. He was pretty sure the tunnel had no other outlets. The only thing left to explore was the other side of the passage.

That raised another concern.

How deep did the cavern go? For all Darius knew, it might take more than a day's travel to search fully. In the past, he had learned the intricacies of each cave, timing his journeys to get back before daybreak and avoid risk. Even though he was older, he was familiar enough to get back in time.

But this new passage might contain anything.

The idea of waiting yet another day was unbearable.

Stroking his chin, Darius looked at the torches he kept on the table. Caution fought with risk. He was an old man, with how many years left? For too long, he had searched fruitlessly, bringing back nothing but questions.

And now he had a lead that he couldn't ignore.

Perhaps it was time to take a bigger risk.

Reaching for a bin underneath the table, he pulled out more torches and laid them on the table next to the others, and then he readied more food.

He wasn't leaving until he found something.

Chapter 38: Neena

EENA AND KAI WERE TIRED and thirsty. For most of the day, they'd ignored their fatigue and pushed on, but now their pace was slowing. Neena looked over the familiar landscape. Occasionally, the land curved up or down in a gradual slope, with long, sandy valleys that gave spectacular views, or with hills that blocked them. Sometimes those views seemed to go on forever, but each came with a toll on their bodies.

Neena's stomach growled. Her throat was parched. She thought about the last meal they'd had — the fawn from the night before. Even that meal was starting to sound appetizing.

Ascending a long upward slope, undoubtedly feeling some of the same exhaustion, Kai asked, "Are we getting close to the shelter where you anticipated staying?"

"It is only a few klicks away," Neena said.

"Good news," Kai said. "Hopefully we can find food there."

"With the cover of shelter, perhaps we can catch some sand rats," Neena said.

Ahead of them, the gradual slope built up to a berm of sand. The natural wall blocked most of the southern landscape, but beyond it, Neena knew, was a downward slope that should make traveling easier. She pushed on, putting one foot in the other. Anxious to reach the shelter, Kai picked up his pace, getting a few steps ahead of her.

He was almost at the crest of the slope when he stopped. The landscape fell deathly quiet.

Neena looked underfoot, certain a rumble would shatter the calm, but Kai watched the berm. She followed his gaze to the top of the hill. Three ratty, staring creatures crept over the wall of sand. Neena looked from their vicious eyes to their spotted coats.

Speckled wolves.

Ribs jutted out from the sides of their gaunt bodies. Their fur was matted and clumped. The wolves stopped, raising their hackles. The lead animal took a slow, offensive step toward Kai, who was closer to the crest of the hill and a more obvious target.

Neena clutched her spear, but even that wouldn't save her, if the wolves decided to attack.

She swallowed as she got her spear in front of her, trying to make herself larger, as her father had taught her. She faced the wolves while avoiding direct eye contact. Kai arched his shoulders.

They both knew better than to run.

The lead wolf bared its teeth, taking another step. Kai held his stance, neither moving, nor breathing. Neena thought about what she'd told Kai. The wolf packs she'd seen rarely bothered humans.

But these wolves must be desperate.

The lead wolf lunged.

Kai cried out as the wolf darted toward him, leapt, and knocked him backward. He managed to throw up an arm before it seized his throat. And then he was on his back. The animal latched onto his sleeve, while Kai's other arm flailed to get up his spear. Following their leader's attack, the other wolves darted in with equal ferocity, snarling and snapping.

"Get away!" Neena screamed.

Of course, the wolves didn't listen.

She cocked back her spear, prepared to throw it, but the

wolves were moving too quickly. She couldn't guarantee she wouldn't hit Kai. Frantic, Neena raced the distance to the vicious animals, whacking the closest with a sideways blow. The animal yelped and retreated. The other wolves weren't giving up as easily. The one on Kai's other side nipped and grabbed at his arm. The lead wolf bit at the spear he'd managed to get in front of his throat.

Raising her spear high in the air, Neena brought it down on the lead wolf's back, screaming. The wolf snarled and yelped, letting go of Kai's arm.

It turned and refocused on Neena.

Neena flailed backward as the wolf crashed into her legs, knocking her off balance and onto her back. Its hot breath and her frantic cries filled the world around her as they landed in a tangle. She turned her spear sideways and shielded her face, listening to the clack of its jaws on the dry piece of wood. From somewhere over the wolf's attack, she heard Kai fighting his own desperate battle.

The lead wolf opened and closed its mouth, finding a mouthful of Neena's sleeve, shaking it back and forth as it searched for flesh. Neena flung up a knee, catching the wolf in the stomach. The wolf doubled down on its biting. She kneed it again, harder.

The wolf cried out and sprang back.

It bared its teeth and arched its back in the sand.

Turning the spear in front of her, Neena leveled the pointed end at the wolf as it leapt again.

Spear met flesh. The wolf yowled.

The sharp stick penetrated the wolf's neck as Neena rolled sideways, carrying wolf and spear to the ground. She lost hold of the spear. Quickly, she scrambled to her feet, getting her hands up defensively, but the creature kicked and squirmed its death throes. Blood spewed around the spear in its neck as it gave a final jerk and went still.

Dislodging her spear, she turned and looked for Kai, her breath hitching in frantic gasps.

Kai had managed to ward the other two wolves away with his spear and was struggling to get to his feet. The hungry animals growled and snarled, regrouping. Drawing her arm back, Neena aimed at the wolf closest to Kai and hurled her spear.

The weapon whizzed through the air, striking her target, but not fatally.

The wolf yelped as the homemade spear lodged in its hindquarters, it took a few erratic steps, and it spun and raced away. The third wolf watched them for a moment before following its brethren, cresting the berm and disappearing from sight.

Catching her breath, Neena made her way to Kai.

"Are you all right?" she asked.

Kai dusted off his clothes as he stood, clutching his spear. She looked down at his arm. The wolf had opened a gash near his wrist, soaking his sleeve with blood. His pants were torn; his hair was disheveled. A few, other rips and tears showed where the wolves had tried getting to him, but he'd managed to avoid more serious damage.

"Your wrist," she said, calling attention to the worst of the injuries.

"I'll be fine," he said, wincing.

"Your wound needs tending," Neena said. "Let's get to the top of the hill, so we can make sure the wolves are gone."

Kai nodded as he looked around at the landscape. Neither needed to voice their other concerns. They were alive, but that might not last long, if something bigger than a wolf had heard them.

Neena and Kai made their way to the top of the berm, hunkering down. From their higher perch, they stared in all directions. They saw no sign of the injured wolf she'd speared, or its companion. The daylight was slowly dying, creating a shimmering glare over the desert. To the north was the long valley of sand they'd left behind. In the opposite direction: more sand.

They heard no rumbles. No Abomination.

They waited in ominous silence for what seemed like a long while. When they were certain no danger imminently lurked, Neena gazed at the spotted wolf farther down the hill that she'd killed.

"The wolf will give us a meal," Kai said, still gasping for breath. "We can dress it and take the meat with us. At the very least, it will save us more hunting."

Neena nodded grimly. She felt no pride in what she'd done. The wolves had done what they needed to survive, just as she had. "I just wish it hadn't taken my spear with it."

Kai held out his arm, showing her the wound on his wrist. Blood fell and splotched the sand. It didn't seem like the type of wound she could sew. Hopefully, it would heal properly. But it needed wrapping.

"Let me clean it," she said, reaching for her flask.

Finding a piece of fabric that the wolf had torn from her sleeve, Neena ripped it off and used it to wrap up his arm, stopping some of the bleeding, after cleaning it with water. Kai thanked her.

"How about you?" he asked. "Are you okay?"

In the frenzy of the encounter, Neena hadn't spent much time checking on herself. She looked down, finding a few scrapes and tears. She didn't see any deep bite marks. Still, she was winded and shaken up, too. When she finished cleaning the wound, they stood and assessed the sandy valley in both directions.

"Hopefully, we have scared the wolves enough that we will not see them again," Neena said.

They traveled the remainder of the day in relative quiet. Kai clutched his spear, while Neena traveled with her knife out. Neena's back was heavy from the wolf meat she had hastily dressed and placed into her game bags. For a while, she had refused Kai's offer to carry it, but finally, he persuaded her to let him shoulder the weight for a klick. He didn't complain as he slung it over his non-injured arm, though a few times she caught him grimacing from the wound she'd bandaged.

The sun was fading over the horizon when he pointed in the distance. "Is that the place of which you spoke?"

Neena nodded as she appraised the shelter in the distance. A long, angular rock the width of many houses sat in the sand. The eastern and western sides sloped up to a higher point in the center, which was about the size of the Comm Building. Underneath, a cave-sized opening allowed light to pass through, leading to a partially enclosed platform made of rock.

"That is the alcove," Neena said, with a nod. "It is where I usually sleep, if I get here late in the day."

The formation was a welcome sight, after so long of travel. And the rock should help keep them safe from the Abomination.

Hopefully.

"How many klicks left to Red Rock?" Kai asked.

"We should be there midday tomorrow," she reiterated.

The thought of actually reaching home seemed surreal. Staring at the familiar formation, Neena could just as easily picture trudging into Red Rock.

"Do others stay here?" Kai asked.

"Sometimes." Neena scanned the distance, wondering if she'd see a billow of smoke from a distant desert fire. The place seemed empty.

No hunters. *No wolves.*

No Abomination.

Neena looked over her shoulder, as if they might see the vicious animals, or the ground parting behind them. All she saw was the setting, glowing sun, looking as magnificent as always.

"Come on," she said. "Let's get to shelter."

Chapter 39: Gideon

"**G**OOD AFTERNOON, SIR."

Gideon nodded as he crossed the main room of the Comm Building, temporarily forgetting about the guard he had stationed there. The Watcher arched his back, stiff from a long day's watch. A flask sat on the ground by his dirty boot.

Gideon looked from the guard to the strong, secure door behind him, leading to the annex. The door was thick enough that it would hold against the prisoner's pounding fists, even if the thief got out of his cell.

"How have things been in here?" Gideon asked, tired from a long day of overseeing the crop disbursement.

"The prisoner yelled for a while, but he's quiet now," the guard said in a low voice. "Horatio and Saurab are in their rooms, resting."

"Why don't you take a break?" Gideon said.

"Thank you, sir." The Watcher gratefully left his post. "I'll fill my flask and be back."

Gideon watched the man cross the room and close the door behind him. He turned his attention to the annex door. The hallway on the other side was silent.

Still, he could never be too careful.

After a moment of quiet, he fished out his key, inserted it in the lock, and swung open the heavy door, revealing the offshoot hallway on the other side. Up and down the long, rectangular corridor, rows of separated rooms lined the walls, cordoned off by thick metal bars. Long, black marks scarred the walls of each of those rooms, where shelves had once hung. As he stepped inside, the smell of rodent scat and sweat clung to his nose.

Gideon peered through the gloom until he found the man The Watchers had captured that afternoon. Huddled by the wall in the second cell, the man looked up with a gaunt face and pleading eyes. Slowly, he rose to his feet and clung to the round, sturdy bars. Gideon appraised him in silence.

When Gideon's eyes became too thick to bear, the man said, "Please. I have a family to feed. I did not mean to steal."

Gideon said nothing. The man was sorry that he was caught. But if he had made it away, that sullen expression would've been an expression of triumph.

"Please…" the man said again.

Watching the captive man, Gideon pictured a slew of others just like him, walking the streets, probably wondering whether they might have made it away. He didn't need anyone getting ideas.

Some of the duller colonists might've welcomed the extra portions of vegetables and roots, but the more intelligent ones—like this man—realized that extra crops meant cuts were coming. It was those people about whom Gideon worried.

Gideon knew how quickly the seeds of discontent could blossom.

One day, food might grow scarce enough that more than a manageable few would consider breaking the rules. How long would it take people to realize their neighbors were better at rationing their meat, or that their crying, starved child might benefit from taking someone else's share? How long would it take for someone to realize they could use their knife to get food in town, instead of food in the desert? Gideon and his men brought a civility that kept them a few steps ahead of chaos, but not much more. The colony's hunger could turn into a starvation that would kill them all.

He, his Heads, and his Watchers numbered only two hundred. His Watchers were decisive, tough men, taught to execute orders and keep people obedient. But they wouldn't stand up against an enormous, unruly mob.

In the aftermath of every storm, it was important that Gideon pay attention to every wandering eye, every uttered word. If his father had taught him anything, it was that weakness led to disorder.

Disorder led to chaos.

He couldn't tolerate either.

"If you behave, I'll let you out in a few days, as I have ordered. Keep talking, and you will be cast out of Red Rock," Gideon threatened, before walking back through the door, leaving the prisoner and the annex behind.

Chapter 40: Neena

NEENA AND KAI BEDDED DOWN under the alcove, on a flat place in the large rock, where the stone was mercifully smooth. Neena was grateful for the shelter, even if it didn't have the full protection of a cave. Despite the open areas behind them, and an overhang that only jutted about fifteen feet over the front edge of the rock, the hard, stone floor spanned a much wider area than where they'd stayed the night before.

It was certainly better than sleeping in the desert.

Looking around, Neena saw a few piles of scattered ashes, and some dried bloodstains, probably from a hunter dressing his kill. On a normal trip, the smoke from her fires would drive away the more curious animals, but of course, they weren't lighting one now.

Handing a blanket to Kai, she asked, "How's your wrist?"

"It's fine," he said.

She inspected his arm in the dying light. Blood had soaked through most of the bandage. It seemed as if the wound was worse than he let on.

"We should clean it again," she told him. "When we get back to Red Rock, our healers can look at it."

Kai winced as he took a seat on his blanket, and Neena huddled next to him, slicing off a piece of the blanket's end so she could use it as fresh gauze. In the last of the sunlight, she treated it again.

"I can't believe how close we are to your colony," Kai said, keeping a brave face as she cleaned off the raw, red skin.

"It seems strange to me, too," Neena said. "It is always an adjustment getting back to my colony, after a while in the desert."

"And it will be even stranger now." Changing to a subject that weighed on both their minds, Kai said, "I wonder how your people will react to me, when we arrive."

"Our story — and your existence — will surprise them," Neena said, drying the wound.

"Just as your existence surprised me."

Neena thought on it. "I'm sure the leaders of Red Rock will have many questions for you, as I have had. Maybe our people can benefit each other."

Kai agreed. It was a hope as much as a question.

Finished cleaning the wound, Neena tied a new bandage over it. The upcoming meeting remained on her mind. She looked over at Kai in the dying sunlight, recalling the time they'd first met. The marks on his head would surely intrigue others, too. She studied the lines that went from his hairline to his temples, which differentiated him from anyone she'd met.

"I don't think I've asked about the marks on your forehead," she said.

"A mark of the heavens," Kai explained, with a smile. "They guide our ascension, after our passing."

"I figured they had meaning," Neena said.

"We get them when we turn of age," he continued. "Our people believe something similar about the heavens as you believe. Although it seems you don't wear the same marks. It is nice to think the pain of this life will mean something, in the end."

"That is a nice thought," Neena agreed.

She smiled. Over the course of the journey, Neena had

developed a surprising concern for Kai. She had acclimated to traveling with him, but she also grew to appreciate his companionship. Hopefully, her people would see through their caution and listen to what he — to what *they* — had to say.

They had positioned so they had a full view of the desert to the south, and also a healthy view to the north, through the rock's round opening. Soon, darkness settled, revealing a sky spackled with stars. They settled back on their blankets, but kept vigilant.

Looking up at those lights, Kai sighed and said, "When I was younger, I used to study the stars and wonder if one of them was Earth."

Neena smiled, feeling a hint of nostalgia. "I used to do the same thing."

"They said the giant, metal objects called ships were probably the size of this rock, or bigger. They said they could travel far greater distances than we can imagine. I always had trouble envisioning them."

Neena smiled. "My brothers used to ask me whether we would ever see one of those strange, metal devices. I told them one day they'd come down, bringing us to a place where we never worried about empty stomachs." She paused as a humorous memory came back to her. "But then I told them, 'If we never had to worry about food, what would we do with our time?'"

Kai laughed softly. "At the very least, we wouldn't have to worry about any monsters like the Abomination," he said.

"Who knows?" Neena shrugged. "Maybe there are worse monsters on other planets."

They stretched their stiff necks and arms, as the night grew colder. Neena pulled out some wolf meat. Together, they shared the gamey, stringy food, which tasted worse than the fawn, but was still edible. Soon, sleep tugged on their weary eyelids.

"We should take shifts watching," Neena suggested. "A better night's rest will serve us well for the remainder of the journey."

"That's a good idea," Kai said. "Why don't you sleep first? If I hear anything, I'll wake you."

Neena looked over at his silhouette in the moonlight. If this had been their first night together, she might've refused, but with some meat in her stomach, enough water, and a warm blanket, Neena felt more secure than she had in days.

She trusted Kai.

She blinked several times, checking the desert and watching his shadow shift as he watched over her. For a moment, she had a fleeting memory of her father, and then she was on the road to sleep.

Her last conscious thought was that they'd reach Red Rock in the morning.

Chapter 41: Raj

RAJ LAY IN A BEDROLL in Helgid's house. For a while, he listened to Samel's quiet shifting, until his brother's breaths grew soft and steady. Helgid rested without a sound, as she usually did.

Raj was alone with his thoughts.

Adriana was stuck in his mind. Thinking of the girl's sad smile made his stomach flutter. He couldn't stop recalling her blues eyes, her long dark hair, or the nice way she'd treated him. And of course, he'd never forget her extraordinary gift.

Raj smiled in the dark as he remembered their conversation over tea.

Adriana was several years older than him, but she was different. She talked to him in the way an adult would. She didn't look down her nose at him, the way some of his neighbors did, or the way the boys did down by the river, when they spoke of his father.

Most of the girls Raj's age were concerned with playing childish games, or huddling close together and whispering.

A few of them were nice, but none took an interest in him beyond a few brief conversations, and certainly none took an interest in his father.

Raj felt a connection with Adriana deeper than sympathy. He felt close to her, because of the losses they'd suffered. He wanted to comfort her, so that she would never feel sad again. Lying in bed, he couldn't stop thinking of the next time he'd see her.

Would she think it strange if he came by tomorrow?

Raj felt embarrassed. Even though he was in the dark, his cheeks flushed and his stomach grew tight. Adriana had invited him back, but he didn't want to be a pest.

Maybe he needed to give it some time.

Or maybe he needed a reason.

Reaching into his pocket, he took out the metal keepsake and turned it over in his hand in the dark. Adriana had already explained everything she knew about it, but maybe she would remember more with another conversation. Maybe together, they could stitch together some clues that would explain the origins of the wondrous object.

At the very least, it was an excuse to talk to her again.

Raj sighed. Perhaps whatever power existed in the heavens had brought them together for a reason. He smiled as the thought stuck in his mind.

He would find her in the morning.

Chapter 42: Darius

ARIUS'S HANDS SHOOK AS HE held on to his cane and his torch. His pulse pounded. Beads of sweat rolled from his brow as he trekked deeper into the auburn cave. He wanted to hurry, crawl faster through the passage he'd found, and emerge out the other side.

He wanted to will the first part of the journey away.

In his bag were five torches—enough to accommodate a long journey, if needed. On the way here, no Watchers had spotted him. Hopefully, that luck would continue.

For the first time in as long as he remembered, Darius felt as if several years of fruitless searching might finally yield something. It felt like tonight, something was special.

A screeching bat took flight from somewhere above him. Darius jolted more than he might normally have, if he hadn't been in such haste. *Slow down*, he told himself. *You don't want to risk a fall.*

Still, some inner force pushed him on.

All at once, he remembered that strange doorway in his dream. Instead of recalling the frightening parts of that nightmare, he recalled Akron's hopeful face and their reconnection. He recalled the joy in his heart at finding his friend alive.

Darius knew better than to believe the lies of sleep, which made glittery promises and ripped them away. Still, some spark drove him.

He traveled the same caves as he had the night before,

winding past the smooth walls, until he reached the narrow passage where he'd first encountered the fox. Darius' heart beat faster as he came across the pile of rocks he'd pulled aside. The passage was still exposed.

Of course, it was.

No one was foolish enough to enter these caves, except Darius.

He swallowed as he crawled through the small opening, feeling the same fear he had the first time about getting stuck, until he was upright and on the other side. This time, he had no decision to make.

Darius turned left.

The cave widened, following a curvy path. His torch light revealed trails of rodent scat. In one corner, he found a small, fresh rat corpse that hadn't yet been ferreted away.

Maybe scavenging animals feared these caves.

He doubted the truth of that paranoid thought—the fox had been here, after all—and yet he couldn't help feeling that way, as the tunnel took a deep, downward slope. Darius tread with careful steps as he avoided scattered rocks and larger, jagged pieces of stone that had broken off the walls. A long, straight gash drew his attention to a nearby part of the tunnel, where a miner had chipped off a piece, long ago.

He'd seen plenty of similar marks before, of course, but it was the first mark in this cave, and that gave him a strange intuition.

A sign?

Darius's hope grew as he moved faster than he should, heading deeper into the tunnels, even farther from the surface and Red Rock. He held his torch higher, lighting his way as small, fast-moving insects scurried into holes. A small cave lizard bolted from the torch light.

A strange smell hit Darius's nose.

The cave smelled dank, old. He kept going until the tunnel broadened and became an enormous, chamber-sized room. The ceiling sloped so high that he couldn't see the top with his torch light, nor could he see the tops of the walls.

Rocks and dust littered his way.

He slowed his steps as he saw something.

Past the rocks, pieces of a strange, gray substance lined the floor. The waste-like material was flaky and ashen.

What was this?

Something gleamed in the light of his torch, pressing him onward.

Darius inched forward, over more of the ash, until he was upon it.

His breath caught in his throat.

A skeleton.

Chapter 43: Darius

D ARIUS KNELT NEXT TO THE skeleton, setting down his torch.

Tattered clothes hung around the yellowed bones. Of course, the flesh was gone. Most of the skeleton was whole, but pieces of it had decayed, or been tugged away by scavenging animals. Darius held his breath and inched closer, guessing that the remains belonged to a medium-sized man or woman.

Or a boy.

Akron?

Darius trembled as he studied the yellowed bones.

The clothing was in so many shreds that it was impossible to tell how the outfit had looked when it was intact. He saw no other clues as to the person's identity, no belongings that would help him make a determination.

Whom had he discovered?

He stared at the old, decayed skeleton, as if the person might get up and answer his questions. But that was as silly as believing in his dream. A sense of failure struck him as he realized his quest might've ended in another question.

And then he noticed a pair of tattered boots on the dead person's feet.

Unlike the shredded pieces of clothing, the leather was intact, save a few holes.

A memory came back to him. All at once, Darius was in his hovel, fixing a spear and listening to Akron speak of one of the recent attacks he'd survived, about a snake that surprised him on a recent trip. The snake had leapt out from a crevice in the one of the tunnels, striking Akron on the tip of one of his boots. At the time, Akron had smiled with youthful exuberance, telling of how he'd escaped the creature. It was easy to smile, once the danger was over and you had survived.

Or maybe he'd wished to impress Darius, who had always been his hero.

Which boot had Akron shown him?

His left.

Darius's heart fluttered as he lifted his torch, until he could see the top of the worn, partially decayed leather.

On top of the left boot, right where he remembered it, were two fang-sized marks.

Akron.

Darius's torch fell from his hands. The wavering flames of his torch illuminated the gaping eye sockets, the jutting ribs, and the decaying bones.

Two years worth of building sadness became a bursting dam of tears.

Akron's happy smile was gone.

This was his end.

Darius collapsed the rest of the way to the ground, sobbing. His quiet gasps became heavy moans, echoing through the enormous chamber. He tried blotting away tears he could no longer stop.

Akron had looked up to him, and Darius had failed him. He should've tried harder to find him, when it counted. He should never have told him about the caves.

I was his hero, and his friend.

And now he's gone.

When he closed his eyes, he could still see the boy's excited face, relaying his discoveries. His trips had been the highlight of his days, just as they had been for Darius.

And now those days were over for both of them.

Sandstorm

Darius cried for Akron's mother, and his father, who had suffered too much, and for too long. He sobbed until he had no more tears to blot on his wrinkled skin, and the last of his crying echoes ceased.

When he was finished, he sat up and stared at the skeleton.

A lingering question came back to him.

Where were Akron's belongings?

Darius looked on either side of the body, but he still saw nothing to answer his previous observation. If Akron had been here, his belongings — his torch — must be close by. Smearing another, final tear, Darius picked up his own torch and looked past the body, intent on exploring the rest of the dark chamber until he found answers.

Akron's parents deserved them.

The room returned to silence.

Darius pulled himself upright and took a step, and then another, wading through more of the flaky black, brown, or grey substance. The vile material caved under his boots. *What was he stepping in?*

He held his torch higher, looking for some obvious clue about Akron's death that he had missed.

He stepped a few feet farther into the chamber.

And stopped.

Darius's mouth hung open as his light revealed dozens of scattered human bones. Most were cracked and broken, covered in the same substance he'd stepped over, or in. Unlike Akron's, none of these bones were in the shape of a skeleton. A fear different from any he had ever known overtook Darius, but he couldn't stop moving.

It felt as if he were in a dream again, and something propelled him.

More and more bones covered the floor; enough that it was impossible to tell how many people he looked at, though he suspected it might be dozens. Darius had never seen so many bodies in one place. Even the worst sandstorms hadn't yielded so many deaths.

He stepped carefully around the vile, long-rotted substance, finding places to put his feet where he wouldn't trip on a bone. He kept his eyes glued to the fringes of his torch light. The chamber was enormous—bigger than the tunnel that preceded it.

Working his way past the bodies, he felt an intense fear.

He couldn't imagine what had done something so horrible.

Darius continued past more of the bones, entering a drier portion of the cave that seemed even wider. His hands shook as he held the torch higher, finding something else in its light. Darius froze. Shards of fear prickled through him.

In front of him was an enormous skeleton—bigger than that of any creature he'd seen, almost the size of the chamber in which he stood. Giant, curved rib bones comprised most of the circular, mammoth remains. Strange, spear-like objects littered the floor underneath the skeleton's center, looking as if they had once been attached. At the front, an enormous round jaw hung open, displaying two gigantic rows of yellowed, jagged teeth.

Each of those teeth was the size of Darius's body.

Slowly, a horror became a realization, as Darius looked over his shoulder in the direction of the human bones, and the vile, rotten substance surrounding them, and back to the remains of the enormous, frightening beast. Somehow, the creature was responsible for their deaths.

Darius trembled.

Chapter 44: Raj

R AJ SNUCK OUT INTO A quiet morning, under the amber glow of the rising sun. Only a few people lingered near their homes, stretching, or staring up at the cliffs. A few cleaned off pushcarts, or quietly washed laundry. Raj looked back at the house, where Helgid and Samel still slept. He wouldn't be gone long enough for them to worry.

Reaching into his pocket, he squeezed the object that Adriana gave him — his excuse to visit her again.

He took the path toward her house, following the same route he'd taken the day before, replaying their conversations in his head. He thought about the memory she'd shared of her grandmother. She'd said that they'd had tea each morning, and she missed it.

Maybe she and Raj could fill that time together.

It was a pleasant thought, and the more Raj turned it in his head, the more he liked it.

Soon he'd reached Adriana's mud brick hovel. The door was closed. Raj looked around the area, noticing a few neighbors tending chores, but he didn't see Adriana. He listened for her voice as he walked slowly past her home. A few muffled voices echoed through the wall.

Probably her mom and dad.

Would they consider it rude if he knocked so early? Raj didn't want to be a pest, nor did he want to annoy some people that he might see often, if he were lucky enough to spend more time with Adriana.

He went past the house, deciding he would come back in a while.

Turning onto the main path past Adriana's alley, he looked right, toward the river. A few people walked toward the bridge in the distance, heading toward the Green Crops. Others stood at the banks, dipping their buckets in the water.

Nearing the river, he studied the slow-moving current. The sun cast a warm glare off the water. Nearby, a mother and father with a toddler splashed and played happily. Seeing that image reminded him of his own parents.

Perhaps he'd visit their graves.

He continued over the well-trodden trail, until the bridge was underfoot. A few people leaned over the rail, looking out over the water, or nodding at him. Off in the distance, Raj studied the rock formations that loomed over the colony, where a few Watchers gazed out over the people below, observing them.

Following the same path as the procession had, he crossed the length of sandy desert, coming around the corner of the western formation and arriving at the field of stones where he'd stood with most of the others the day before.

Three people huddled by a gravestone.

Raj picked a diagonal path, cutting past them, curving by some half-buried grave markers. Using memory to guide him, he counted them, until he reached the stones marking his parent's graves.

Raj put his palms on the ground, kneeling close enough that the other people couldn't hear him.

"Hi Mom. Hi Dad," he said quietly. "I miss you."

Raj swallowed, as an unexpected sadness hit him.

"Neena is still out hunting," he whispered, speaking around the lump in his throat. "I'm hoping she's okay, after the sandstorm. I'm doing what I can to take care of Samel, like you would've wanted. And Helgid is helping us, too."

He felt a pang of grief. It felt as if he were speaking to his parents, instead of mounds of dirt. Or that's what he told himself, whenever he had conversations like this. Raj sighed, looking between the two graves, focusing on his father's empty one.

Raj remembered the ceremony they'd had for Dad. At the time, he had felt too strange to cry.

When he closed his eyes, he could still remember those first few weeks after his father left, lying in his bedroll and wondering if his father would return. That made him remember all the times he'd asked Neena about it. The more that Raj thought about her answer, the more certain he became that Neena had held something back.

Maybe he would ask her about it again.

Blotting away a few tears before they fell, Raj got to his feet.

A fist struck him in the back.

Pain seared through Raj's body.

Several rough hands threw him to the ground, near his father's hard grave marker. More than one person knelt, rolled him over, and pinned him. Raj struggled and screamed, but a hand clamped over his mouth. Through the glare of the sun, he saw four figures surrounding him: the boy with the pointed nose, a stern-faced boy, a shaggy-haired kid, and a tall one.

Bailey's boys.

Frantic, Raj looked for the people he'd seen earlier, but they were gone. The Watchers were on the other side of the cliffs, out of sight. Of course, they were. Bailey and his boys had picked this moment on purpose.

Bailey walked out of the glare, standing over him with a sneer.

"What are you going to do now, orphan boy?" he spat.

Raj tried lashing out with his arms and legs, but the kids held them.

"I told you this wasn't over," Bailey said.

Leaning down, Bailey plucked Raj's knife from its sheath and held it up in the sunlight, examining the blade, as his eyes lowered back to Raj.

"Did you come out here to cry, like a sissy?"

The others laughed.

"He came out here to cry over his dead dad," said the kid with the pointed nose. "Maybe he wanted to ask him why he didn't leave sooner."

The boys laughed harder.

Raj screamed into one of the sweaty hands over his mouth. He squirmed and bucked. He spat every foul word he knew, even though no one could hear him. He wouldn't let them intimidate him, even if it meant his death.

"Maybe we can cut out your eyeballs, so you won't have to cry anymore," Bailey said with a smile, lowering Raj's knife toward his face.

New fright bit through Raj's stomach. His hands and legs coursed with an instinct to flee, to fight, but he could do nothing except watch Bailey lower the knife. Bailey got within a few inches of Raj's cheek, twisting and turning the blade.

"Wait," one of his friends interrupted. "I found something."

Bailey looked up, distracted. "What is it?"

The kid with the pointed nose said, "I'm not sure. It's in his pocket."

"Make sure he doesn't move," Bailey ordered. "I'll see what it is."

Bailey fished a filthy hand into Raj's pocket, digging around until he found the item to which the other kid had drawn attention. Triumph lit Bailey's face as he pulled out Adriana's round keepsake. He held up the object, inspecting its surface and turning it over, rubbing at the indents with his thumb.

Raj yelled harder into the hand over his mouth, screaming for Bailey to put it down, but his words were muted. A new joy took over Bailey's face as he saw the anger in Raj's eyes. Each muffled word prompted more interest.

"Was this your daddy's?" Bailey asked.

Raj screamed a curse word into the hand stifling his mouth. Of course, he wouldn't tell them the truth. He wouldn't tell them anything.

"Maybe it belongs to that old woman he hangs around with," said the taller kid. "Maybe she smooths out her wrinkles with it."

A few more kids laughed.

"Whatever it is, I like it," Bailey said, as he made a show of turning it over. "Maybe I'll keep it."

A worry crossed the pointed-nosed kid's face as he looked past Bailey, up toward the cliffs.

"He might go to The Watchers. He might say you stole it."

Something that looked like worry flashed through Bailey's face. "You wouldn't go to The Watchers on me, would you?" Bailey asked Raj. Lowering the keepsake, he held the knife to his neck. "'Cuz if you did, I would make sure it would be the last words you spoke."

Raj tried sucking in a breath to shout again, but he couldn't find any air.

"What does it do, anyway?" the tall kid asked, curiosity crossing his face as he leaned over Raj to take a look at the keepsake.

Bailey shrugged. "I don't know. I think it's just pretty."

"I think it would look prettier as a knife, or a spear-tip," said the boy with a smirk.

"I don't know, Bailey," said the boy with the pointed nose. "What if someone catches you before you melt it down?"

Bailey thought on that for a moment. Indecisiveness went through his face, before he arrived at a decision. "Maybe I'll bury it where no one can find it, so the orphan boy won't squeal. And I'll bury his knife, too."

Raj screamed uselessly.

"I said I owed you for what you did at the river," Bailey said, his indecisiveness turning into a grin. "And I meant it." Holding up the knife and the keepsake, he said, "Consider these payment, for threatening me."

Bailey's triumphant smile grew wider.

Without warning, he socked Raj in the stomach.

The rest of the wind escaped from Raj's body.

Bailey punched him several more times, hitting his ribs and his chest, until Raj's eyes blurred with watery pain. He kept hitting him, until flashes of light blinked through Raj's eyes.

And then the hands released Raj, and he gasped to regain his breath.

"If you follow us or say a word, you'll regret it," Bailey spat. "And so will Samel."

Raj wheezed a retort no one could hear.

The boys walked away.

Through the sun's glare, Raj saw their silhouettes making their way back through the gravesite. A few looked over their shoulders as they left, snickering.

And then they were around the cliffs, and out of sight.

My knife.

My keepsake.

Raj struggled for breath. He pushed with all his strength, managing to get to his feet. His ribs and stomach ached so badly he thought he would collapse. His lungs screamed.

He staggered through the sand, barely putting one boot in front of the other. Each footfall brought new pain. Several times, he almost collapsed, but he managed to make it a ways from the graveyard and around the rock formation, catching sight of Bailey and his gang passing the Green Crops and heading for the bridge. Raj opened his mouth to cry out, but he produced only a muffled cry.

Halfway across the bridge, the boys stopped.

Helplessly, Raj watched Bailey lean over the side of the bridge, look in a few directions, and drop two small objects into the river.

Pain flashed behind Raj's eyes again.

He collapsed.

He didn't move.

Chapter 45: Neena

"**W**E'RE ALMOST THERE," NEENA SAID, pushing faster.

She shielded her eyes from the sun's glare. For most of the morning, she and Kai had trekked without stopping, leaving behind the alcove that had sheltered them for the night. Now, they traveled a landscape with rugged hills, covered in sparse vegetation and infrequent, craggy red rocks. Those rocks served as landmarks when Neena hunted. Each formation brought her a wave of nostalgia, as she looked at them.

She couldn't remember a time when she'd missed Red Rock more.

Too often on this trip, she'd been certain she wouldn't return. And now the trip was ending.

Kai smiled, wiping some sweat from his brow. "I won't lie, it will be nice to finish this journey and get to your colony."

Neena nodded and readjusted the bag on her back.

Still, she was anxious.

She couldn't stop thinking about what she'd say to her leaders. Too many words threatened to spill out of her mouth, as she tried putting the experience of several days into a story they'd understand.

The only times she'd been in close quarters to Gideon and his men was at her parents' funerals, or a few gatherings. The Red Rock leaders made her nervous in a way that even the hunt did not. Their presence signified order and fear. And now, she had to address them with news that might be unbelievable, at least in the case of the monster.

She looked for hunters, or other silhouettes far away on the border of the ground and sky, but she saw nothing, other than a few roaming insects and some sand rats.

Hoping to distract from her nerves, Neena pointed at a few of the familiar rock formations.

"Do you see that one?" she asked, gesturing at a rock formation with two, spear-like pieces sprouting from the top. "Once I found a male Rydeer at its base."

Kai nodded as he appraised where she pointed. "Did you catch it?"

"I speared it shortly after I saw it," Neena explained. "That was one of the shortest trips I've taken." Farther along, Neena pointed out another rock formation. "I hid next to that rock once, during a lesser sandstorm, a year ago."

"I see."

Passing a pair of small, ragged hills, Neena recalled how spectacular the view had seemed when she was younger. She didn't bother voicing her story, due to her increasing nervousness.

"Will we see your colony soon?" Kai asked, noting Neena's quicker pace.

"Yes," Neena confirmed. "We should see more familiar landmarks once we crest this hill."

Her feet couldn't take her fast enough as they hiked up the last incline that stood between her and Red Rock. She envisioned Raj and Samel at home, probably waiting for her, or helping Helgid with chores. At the moment, a meal with her family felt like a gift from the heavens.

They crested the hill.

Dozens of tall, auburn rock spires rose in the air, like spears dropped from the sky. Some of the tall, pinnacle-like formations were as thin as the width of several people, while others were even wider. All rose majestically into the sky, with smooth, unclimbable sides. Most were red, with hints of brown and orange.

Eventually, the spires segued to a patch of sandy desert, where two final spears sat like two sides of an enormous, natural door. Through the gap between them, rising high above on the horizon, were the enormous stone walls that protected Neena's colony, and the canyon in the middle, where her people's homes were nestled. The sight of those tiny, distant homes gave Neena a wave of nostalgia.

"This is Red Rock," Neena told Kai. "This is my home."

Chapter 46: Neena

NEENA AND KAI TREKKED BETWEEN the rock spires, taking the most direct route, until they reached the last batches of them, passing between the two that looked like a natural entrance.

Kai looked beyond them with awe.

A slew of distant, tiny homes and buildings came into better view, tucked between the rock wall barriers in the canyon. Neena appraised the mud brick homes, and several wider buildings in front, which were the tithing buildings and the storehouses. Tiny figures milled in front of them, or on the main path that cut through the colony center. More people traveled between the hovels.

Her people were alive.

"They survived the sandstorm," she said, with more relief than she ever remembered feeling.

Wonder clung to Kai's face as he looked at the homes and the formations, but mostly at the colonists. "It is unbelievable to see so many people that I never knew existed."

Neena smiled. She'd feel the same way, if the situation were reversed.

Eventually, they closed within a hundred feet of the front row of buildings.

Neena looked between the tithing buildings and storehouses. The large, wide doors of the tithing houses hung open, as they usually did during the day, when hunters came in to count their game. Inside those buildings, she saw the familiar, long wooden tables, where a few burly men she recognized chatted with some hunters.

Down the main path, several people glanced over, noticing them. Most turned away, until they realized something unusual.

Their attention returned to Kai.

Neena looked over at her companion. At a closer glance, anyone with eyes could see his darker clothing, and the symbols on his head.

Neena swallowed as more and more people tapped their friends' shoulders, joining what was quickly becoming a larger audience. A few of the hunters in the tithing buildings turned from their conversations or their tables to look through the wide doors. Children pointed and whispered as Neena and Kai got close enough to verify Kai was a stranger.

Fear crossed their faces.

They were scared of him. And they were scared of her, too, because she was with him.

All at once, Neena remembered the whispers that surrounded that visit with the strangers, when she was a child.

The decision to warn her people had been much easier when she was out in the desert, frantically trying to make it back. Now that she'd gotten here, she had no idea how to proceed. She wanted to yell warnings and shout her story to anyone who might listen, but inciting a panic wouldn't help anyone. She recalled Kai's words.

Panic is the easiest road to death.

They kept walking, until they reached the head of the main path. Before she could consider the next step of a plan, five men worked their way through the crowd, cutting toward them.

The Watchers.

Of course, they'd seen them coming.

Neena's apprehension became a thick pit in her stomach as the men strode with importance, holding their spears.

"Wait here," she told Kai, as they halted at the cusp of the main path and waited for the men to approach.

Out of the corner of her eye, Kai tensed. Neena kept her head straight and her focus on the oncoming men, waiting until they were close before she cleared her throat and said, "We need to speak with Gideon."

Chapter 47: Gideon

GIDEON SAT AT THE TABLE in the center of the Comm Building, staring at the round, metal centerpiece. His Heads of Colony sat all around him. Plates of food lined the table, remnants of the meal they'd had over their discussion of the crops. All around him, his men chatted and held private conversations, finished with the important business of the meeting.

The door burst open.

Thorne and a Watcher entered.

Heads turned as the rest of the people around the table sensed that something of importance was happening. The two men took quick, purposeful strides toward Gideon.

Getting within a few feet of the table, Thorne stopped and announced, "Someone is here to speak with you, Gideon."

Feeling the weight of all the eyes in the room, Gideon asked, "Who?"

"A hunter girl, returning from the desert." Thorne's voice took a grave turn as he added, "She is one of ours, but she is with a strange man. We think he might be from New Canaan."

The last of the conversations ceased as people heard the last of those words, and processed them.

An unexpected dread rose in Gideon's stomach. "We told their people to stay away. We told them not to visit us again."

Thorne remained quiet. It wasn't his question to answer.

Gideon looked between the worried eyes of Wyatt, Brody, Saurab, and Horatio. They all knew what had been discussed.

"Is he one of the people with whom we met?" Gideon asked.

"No, he is a strange man, whom we have never seen," Thorne said. Turning to the other people in the room, he addressed them all. "He wears the markings of his people."

Chapter 48: Neena

EENA AND KAI STOOD ON the edge of the dirt path. Almost a hundred people streamed from their homes, gathering on the main path from the mouths of the alleys, fighting for a better view of what was surely a scene that none would soon forget. Most kept a cautious distance, watching and waiting. Three of the five Watchers remained in front of Neena and Kai, holding their weapons cautiously as they waited for the leaders.

Neena and Kai had already handed over their spear and knife.

Now, they waited.

Glancing up at the cliffs, Neena saw more Watchers turned in her direction. She had never felt more pairs of eyes on her. It felt as if she were standing in front of a procession, or leading one of the colony's ceremonies. She wanted to push through the growing crowd, find Raj and Samel, and make sure they were safe. She wanted to forget about the message she had come to relay.

In just a few short moments, she had transformed from a lowly girl whom no one respected to a person off of whom no one could take their eyes.

Commotion from farther down the path drew her attention. Men, women, and children parted. Some of the whispers grew quiet, as a new group emerged, striding with importance.

Gideon, his Heads of Colony, and more Watchers.

Gideon and his men took a few confident steps ahead of the others, stopping in front of Neena and Kai.

Neena swallowed as she faced a row of leaders she'd never met alone. She looked between them for a moment, her nervousness growing as she surveyed their stern faces.

She focused on Gideon.

Gideon's steely gaze felt even more severe up close. His gray, slicked-back hair spoke of his years of leadership and knowledge. For all of her life, Neena had known him as the face of Red Rock, making decisions and giving orders, but she had never captured his individual attention. Standing before him now — with so many colonists watching, as well as his Heads of Colony — felt surreal.

Clearing her throat, mustering up her courage, Neena said, "We need to speak with you in private."

Gideon watched her, silently judging, as was the crowd.

For a moment or longer, no one spoke. The Watchers looked as if they awaited an order, or perhaps another word from Neena or Kai. The crowd shifted from foot to foot. To Neena's surprise, Gideon turned and addressed Kai.

"Where did you come from?"

Kai shifted uncomfortably under the glare of so many eyes. He sucked in a breath. "I'm from a colony called New Canaan."

A murmur of disbelief made its way through the crowd. Gideon and Wyatt, one of his Heads of Colony, exchanged an unreadable glance.

"I was out hunting, when Neena found me," Kai continued, filling the uncomfortable silence. "I got lost in a sandstorm. Neena helped me."

The Heads of Colony turned to Neena, as if she might refute his story. "I found him when he was nearly dehydrated," she confirmed.

"You should've let him die," Gideon said coldly.

The crowd gasped as if they'd been struck. Mothers recoiled, hiding their children.

Before Neena could voice her confusion, Gideon raised an arm.

"Detain them!" he yelled, shocking everyone with his unexpected command.

Neena's heart pounded.

A small army of Watchers rushed past Gideon and The Heads of Colony, in Neena and Kai's direction. Neena threw her hands up, but not before several pairs of rough, grabbing hands locked on her arms and shoulders, clenching her tightly. Kai kicked and yelled as a group of men violently took hold of him, taking no care for his wounded wrist.

"What's going on, Neena?" he shouted. "What are they doing to us?"

Panic rose in her stomach as she realized she had no answer. Neena looked between the crowd and Gideon, suddenly feeling as if she was the stranger, or that some waking nightmare had taken hold of her.

"I don't understand!" Neena protested, looking between Gideon, his Heads of Colony, and his Watchers. "What's happening?"

"Let me go!" Kai yelled, as the men jostled him.

Hearing Kai's screams of pain and protest, Gideon turned angry. "Silence that man! Bring him to the annex. That criminal doesn't deserve to walk among us."

"Criminal? What are you talking about?" Neena asked.

"Neena! Tell them I mean no harm!" Kai yelled.

Ignoring his pleas, The Watchers dragged Kai kicking and screaming up the path, where the surprised bystanders leapt from the way, gasping in fright and disbelief.

Before Neena could defend herself or explain further, Gideon jabbed a finger at her and yelled, "Take her, too! She can join him in jail!"

SANDSTORM BOOK 2 COMING SOON!

Afterword

Hopefully, the planet of Ravar feels as real to you as it does to me. I've had a blast creating both the world and the characters for this series.

The creature in SANDSTORM was inspired, at least in part, by a legendary creature called the Minhocão, from South American culture. Reportedly seventy-five to a hundred and fifty feet long, the earthworm-like cryptid burrowed through the ground, feasting on animals above the surface and leaving deep trenches in its wake. Purportedly, the creature's girth was wide enough to collapse houses, destroy swaths of farmland, and even divert rivers.

If you are looking for a scare, an Internet search will give you an idea of the size and appearance of the creature. A highway was even named after it in Sao Paulo, Brazil.

Of course, I added some of my own features, like the creature's "quills", which are based on an earthworm's setae, allowing it to tunnel through the ground, and its fetid secretions.

As you have seen, there is more to unveil about the people of Red Rock, the Abomination, and especially Kai.

If you enjoyed Sandstorm Book 1, please leave a review! Reviews are like torches, leading Darius out of a dark, harrowing cave.

As always, thanks for reading! Book 2 will be out in August 2018!

Tyler Piperbrook
June 2018

Email & Facebook

If you're interested in getting an email as soon as **SAND-STORM 2** comes out, sign up here: **http://eepurl.com/qy_SH**.

You'll periodically get updates on other books but no spam. Unsubscribe at any time.

If you'd like to get a bit more involved, you can find me on **Facebook** at:

http://www.facebook.com/twpiperbrook

Other Things To Read

Since Book 2 of SANDSTORM isn't out yet...
The **CONTAMINATION** series might tide you over. It's a fast-paced, zombie apocalypse story. You can get it on all retailers now!

Made in the USA
Monee, IL
07 March 2022

92440376R00122